May God bless you with many Golden Memories! Linda Lewis

Golden Memories

A Timeless Story of First Love and Enduring Friendship

LINDA ANN LEWIS

ISBN 978-1-64079-386-6 (Paperback)
ISBN 978-1-64079-387-3 (Digital)

Christian Faith Publishing, Inc.
296 Chestnut Street
Meadville, PA 16335
www.christianfaithpublishing.com

Printed in the United States of America

In loving memory of my mother
Norma Jean (Griffin) Gee

and my grandmother
Lucille J. (Van Wagnen) Throop

For the Lord is good;
His steadfast love endures forever,
and his faithfulness to all generations.
—Psalm 100:5

Acknowledgments

My thanks to:

- My husband, Bill Lewis, who has been supportive, encouraging, and who helped me with various land and property searches; one of which was locating the original Bailey farm.

- My daughter, Katie Heid, who took time from her busy family life and work as a teacher, public speaker, journalist, and ministry leader, to encourage my writing and help me with editing.

- My friend, Karen Conover, author, and mentor, who gave me a great critique and editing advice. She had such insight and inspired me to continue to improve and publish my stories.

- My mother, Norma Gee, for some firsthand accounts of Henry and Ethel's home and life from her memory of living with them as a child. She also furnished pictures, documents, and information from the family Bible. My mother was the gentle light of our family and a true inspiration of love and patience to me. She led me to Jesus Christ when I was a child, and for that, I am eternally grateful.

Contents

Preface

The original journal entitled *Golden Memories* is a handwritten account by my great-grandmother, Ethel Van Wagnen, surrounding the events she shared with her dear friend, Grafton Gawne.

More than a list of events, her writing is a window into the past; a key unlocking family history in the kind of detail rarely shared and preserved for future generations.

More than names, dates of birth, and deaths on a family tree chart, it reveals facts about daily life, names of friends, town events, and local trips with details down to what they ate for supper and what time the family retired to bed.

More importantly, the journal shares the feelings of my great-grandmother as a forty-eight-year-old woman living in the 1920s. It tells what she experienced day to day in her family relationships, some disappointments, and feelings about faith, love, and dealing with loss.

Reading between the lines, you might conclude some other things, such as regrets or secrets from the past.

I don't know if my great-grandmother's journals were meant for others to read. I believe she wrote them to document the happy times spent after reuniting with her childhood friend, Graff, and then she hand-copied an exact duplicate, including the Kodak photos, to present to Graff as a gift. That is why, with the permission of my mother, Norma Gee, I carefully and respectfully pass them on.

Originally, three journals were written, but not all the entries are included in this story. I have preserved the heart of her writings and attempted to keep the entries as she wrote them, while maintaining her style when I added other information. *Golden Memories* is a blend of fact and fiction and many details were left to my imagination.

In one particular line in Ethel's journal, she seemed to be longing back to her girlhood days. Those words sparked my interest to write about those days, and it became a perfect place to add chapters "Looking Back to the 1880s." That was the moment I began a journey of discovery, personal challenge, and desire to share my Christian faith through the stories.

With no other information about that time in her life except a few hints I picked up on in her journals, I embarked on extensive research. To attempt to be as historically accurate as possible, I searched family ancestries for many generations, did multiple family census searches, gathered over a hundred old photos, checked county and township records, discovered newspaper archives of articles and obituaries, and read Historical Societies records. I also gained information from the family Bible and got vital firsthand accounts from my mother. The amount of material I compiled from this research was considerable and too much to be added to the story. In order to be able to share this, I have included some of this background information in the Afterword—notes pages at the end of the book.

In gathering all this information, my research and writings stretched over five years and became more urgent to complete when my mother began to show signs of dementia. I so wanted her to be able to read and enjoy the published book of all of my work and her personal input. As I pushed to get it published, my mother was diagnosed with terminal cancer.

My original goal was to publish the works of my great-grandmother and to make my writings blend with hers to tell a story I believe may have occurred. What I ended with can truly be called a "labor of love."

Chapter 1 and the stories of Ethel's girlhood are my writings. I have attempted to answer some questions about what happened to the childhood friendship of Ethel and Graff through the years. As you read, you will notice the chapters change back and forth from the 1920s to the 1880s, so it becomes two stories in one.

Filling in the blanks of someone's life is risky at best and presumptive to believe I might get it right more than 130 years later. But I hope that Ethel would be pleased with the finished work that she so lovingly composed.

So, it is with humility that I offer these writings. I pray that they will be a blessing to anyone who reads them.

Linda Ann Lewis

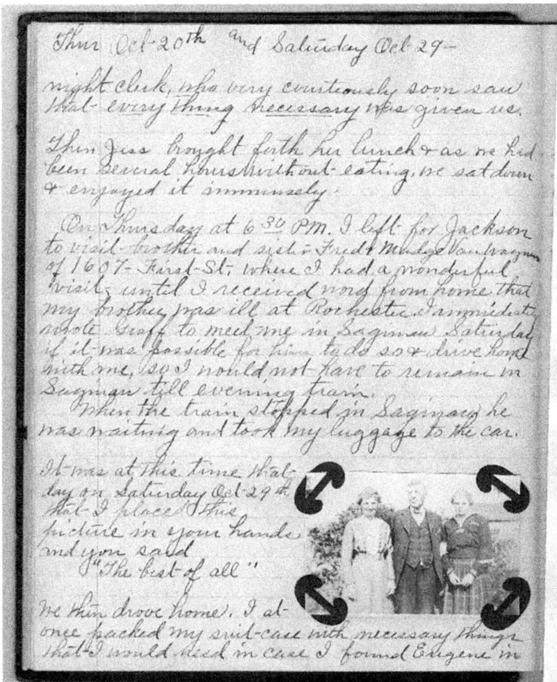

Thur Oct 20th and Saturday Oct 29 -

night clerk, who very courteously soon saw that every thing necessary was given us.

Then Jess brought forth her lunch & as we had been several hours without eating, we sat down & enjoyed it immensely.

On Thursday at 6 30 PM. I left for Jackson to visit brother and sister Fred & Madge Vanwagner of 1607 - First St. where I had a wonderful visit until I received word from home that my brother was ill at Rochester. I immediately wrote Graff to meet me in Saginaw Saturday if it was possible for him to do so & drive home with me, so I would not have to remain in Saginaw till evening train.

When the train stopped in Saginaw he was waiting and took my luggage to the car.

It was at this time that day on Saturday Oct 29th that I placed this picture in your hands and you said "The best of all"

We then drove home. I at once packed my suit-case with necessary things that I would need in case I found Eugene in

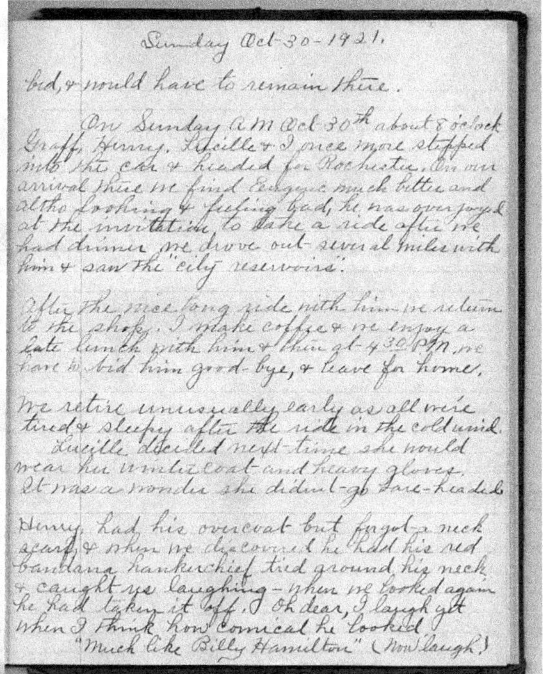

Sunday Oct 30 - 1921.

bed, & would have to remain there.

On Sunday A.M. Oct 30th about 8 o'clock Graff, Henry, Lucille & I once more stepped into the car & headed for Rochester. On our arrival there we find Eugene much better and altho looking & feeling bad, he was overjoyed at the invitation to take a ride after we had dinner we drove out several miles with him & saw the "city reservoirs".

After the nice long ride with him we return to the shop. I make coffee & we enjoy a late lunch with him & then at 4 30 P.M. we have to bid him good-bye, & leave for home.

We retire unusually early as all were tired & sleepy after the ride in the cold wind.

Lucille decided next time she would wear her winter coat and heavy gloves. It was a wonder she didn't go bare-headed.

Henry had his overcoat but forgot a neck scarf, & when we discovered he had his red bandana handkerchief tied around his neck & caught us laughing - when we looked again he had taken it off. Oh dear, I laugh yet when I think how comical he looked "Much like Billy Hamilton" (Now laugh)

Original pages from Ethel's journals.

The Families

Vassar, Michigan—circa 1888

Bailey Family	*Age*
Husband: John	60
Wife: Lucy Jane	56
Children	
Gene (Alfred Eugene)	24
Ella	22
Ethel	15

Gawne Family	
Husband: Alfred	42
Wife: Olive	33
Children	
Grafton	18
Alma	16
George	13
Cyrus	11
Laura	9
Alfred	7
Olive	5
Myrtle	3
Bertha	baby

Millington, Michigan—1921

Van Wagnen Family	*Age*
Husband: Henry	51
Wife: Ethel	49
Children	
Lucille	22
Willard	17
John (wife Maybelle)	27
Mrs. Thalia (Blackmer)	24
Her family: Husband, Vilas	27
Daughter Theo	3
Son Billy	2

Chapter 1
Lizzie

Midland Township, Michigan
July 23, 1920
Barnyard of the Gawne Family Farm

Grafton Gawne bent over his hay wagon and gave the sideboard another pull. The heat and humidity of the late afternoon was starting to wear on him. It was hot, sticky work getting the bed of the wagon back into shape, but it needed to be fixed. As with most jobs on the farm, you didn't plan it; you just "get 'er done." Years of hauling who knows how many stacks of hay had taken its toll. There would soon be another crop to get loaded, and this wagon was going to be filled to the brim.

Graff had been working hard on farms since his childhood. He left school after the sixth grade and started putting in a man's day's work with his father, which was nearly forty years ago. Now he had his own place with his wife Lizzie, who was in the barn now finishing up some chores and milking the cows.

He wiped his sweaty forehead with the back of his shirtsleeve and stood up. In looking at the western sky past the barn, he noticed the darkening storm clouds. He had been hearing rumbling thunder for a while but hadn't looked up to see how strange the sky was now. He just took a deep breath of the warm air and went back to work on the wagon.

Lizzie Gawne stood just inside the wide-open doors of the barn. The air inside the barn was stifling with the heat mixed with the smell of animals and manure. She had a half-filled bucket of milk in her hand and was headed for the last cow when she stopped to look out at the barnyard. She watched her husband, Graff, as he worked on the old hay wagon and thought to herself, *I hope he finishes that soon. Rain is comin' in for sure.*

Just then, she heard the footsteps of her young companion, Johnny Snyder, running up behind her. "Miss Lizzie," he gasped excitedly, "can I go pet the horses?" His face was flushed and sweaty from all his activities.

"Of course, but not too much longer. The weather looks real stormy, and we don't want to get caught out here in a downpour," Lizzie warned.

"All right, I'll hurry," the boy said as he turned and ran back past the cows toward the horse stall.

Little John, as some called him, was here for a visit with his parents Pearl and Ivah. He had practically lived in the barn for the past two days, exploring every corner and checking out all the animals. The horses were his favorite. He was eleven years old, with dark brown hair and eyes, and a boy always looking for something to explore. He reminded Lizzie of her own son, Thomas, at that age. Thomas was grown now, twenty-three and married with a precious son of his own. Even though her grandson was just a few months old, Lizzie wondered if he might end up being called Little Thomas or Tom Jr. She smiled at the thought of the baby that gave her so much joy.

The sound of rumbling thunder brought her thoughts back to the task at hand. One more cow to milk and they would head back to the house. The boy's mother, her dear friend Ivah, was in the house working on supper. It was a treat for Lizzie to have another woman to help her with the chores and keep her company. Ivah had told her that she wasn't much for the farmwork, but she would be happy to help with all the meals. That suited Lizzie just fine.

The air was still and the sky overhead darkening when Graff gave the wagon a few more hits with a hammer. He was just about done with the work on the wagon when he noticed something strange. The hair on his arms and neck began to prickle. He quickly stood up in alarm and dropped his hammer. Suddenly, a loud crack of lightning hit the ground in front of the barn door. Graff was shocked to see the bright bolt as it struck so close, and he heard the sound of whinnies from the frightened horses as he took off running toward the barn. When he reached the doorway, he almost tripped over Lizzie, who was lying on the floor on her side. The bucket was overturned near her with the milk spilling out. He bent down to his wife and turned her to see her face, then reached his arms around her and pulled her lifeless body up and held her to him.

"No, don't go, Lizzie, oh god no!" His heart felt like it was pounding out of his chest, but hers was silent.

For a few moments, he held her, and then through his tears, he looked down the way near the first cow stable and saw Johnny lying on the floor. His eyes were fixed on the boy as he laid Lizzie back down. He stumbled over to the boy and knelt down beside him, knowing at once that Johnny was dead too. He placed his hand on the boy's small chest and felt no life in him. As Graff lingered beside him, he heard the sounds of the restless animals, the rumbling thunder, and rain spattering in the barnyard.

Suddenly, Graff heard footsteps running toward the barn. He stood up and faced the doorway as Pearl Snyder, the boy's father, rushed in and saw Lizzie.

"Johnny?" he asked. With a shocked look on his face, he stepped toward Graff who instinctively stood to shield Pearl from seeing his son. The two men's eyes met, and as Pearl stepped toward him, Graff took him by the shoulders and held him for a moment. But Pearl had already seen Johnny's body and pushed past Graff to kneel beside his son.

Just then, Johnny's mother, Ivah, came running into the barn. She looked down at Lizzie and then spotted her husband. "Johnny!" she screamed as she ran past Graff. He didn't try to stop her. The parents were overcome with grief and cried their son's name over and over.

Graff slowly trudged back to Lizzie and dropped to his knees beside her and held her in his arms once again before kissing his sweet wife good-bye.

Millington, Michigan—July 31, 1920

Henry Van Wagnen quickly walked down the sidewalk toward his house. It was a very warm summer day, perfect for a stroll through the quiet, little town he resided in. But today, Henry's heart was heavy, and he took no pleasure in this short walk. He had made a special trip three blocks to the drugstore to pick up the newspaper requested by his wife, Ethel. He held it close to him firmly under his arm and didn't open it. That would be for Ethel to do, considering the news inside it.

The quiet streets were sheltered by large oak and maple trees, whose branches nearly touched the ones growing on the other side of the street. Henry glanced at the treetops as he approached the railroad tracks that ran through the east part of town. The trains carried grain from the nearby elevators south to Detroit, and north to Saginaw, Midland and beyond. They also carried passengers and connected families with their loved ones who lived a good distance away. The townspeople had become accustomed to the daily sounds of the long whistles and clackity-clack. Children often waited near the tracks to watch the massive engines roll by, wave to the engineer, and wait for the sight of the caboose that marked the end of the train.

Henry stepped gingerly over the tracks and his thoughts returned to his somber errand. Just two more blocks until he reached home. He passed the houses on the streets that he knew so well. Many of the residents inside were friends, and he would normally look toward them as he passed by, to wave or stop for a short visit; but not today. There was not time, and he really didn't feel like talking about the latest weather, family illnesses, and the like.

Just then, he approached the Henderson home and saw Mrs. Henderson in her side yard hanging up her washing. It appeared she was almost done since the clotheslines were nearly full. She had a couple of clothespins in her mouth as she reached the tail of a man's shirt and pressed a pin to hold it. As she spotted Henry, she pulled the other pin out and smiled to begin a friendly conversation. But he gave a quick wave and continued walking. Mrs. Henderson must have sensed her neighbor wasn't very talkative this morning. She gave a nod his way and continued her chore.

Henry quickened his steps as he turned the corner on East Street and drew near to his home. He dreaded the thought of the painful news he was bringing and sighed as he came to his front gate and walked through. He followed the short path and went up the steps to the wooden porch and opened the screen door. It squeaked its familiar greeting as it closed behind him.

Wiping his feet on the rug just inside the door, he hung his hat on the hook of the hall tree that stood on his left. Ahead of him was the large oak dining room table and chairs and the old coal stove that kept the home warm during the long winter months. He wanted to linger a moment in these pleasant, familiar surroundings, but he knew he couldn't. Henry took a few steps and turning to his left entered the parlor.

Inside, on the sofa, sat his wife Ethel waiting with a serious look on her face. Their grown daughter, Lucille, sat in a chair across from her mother, and both women seemed frozen to their seats as he entered the room. Henry walked over to Ethel and handed her the copy of *The Midland Sun* dated July 29, 1920.

Henry stood by the sofa as Lucille jumped up to join him. They waited in silence as Ethel opened the paper and scanned the front page. It didn't take long to spot what she dreaded to find. Right in the middle of the page was the word *Obituary*.

"Oh," Ethel moaned, "here it is." Lucille leaned in closer.

"Read it out loud, Mama."

"Yes, dear, read it to us," echoed Henry. Ethel sighed and then began.

Gawne

The funeral of Mrs. Elizabeth Gawne, whose sudden death from a stroke of lightning last Friday, shocked the whole community, took place from the farm home on the Bay City road Sunday afternoon. In charge were the Rebekahs, of which she was a member. The remains were taken by auto to Vassar, her childhood home for burial. Mrs. Sarah McKeen, her aged mother, brothers James and William of Vassar, sisters Mrs. Mabel Lintz of Bay City and Mrs. Ella Smith of Vassar were all present at the funeral.

Ethel paused a moment to compose herself and then continued to read.

Snyder

The funeral service for Johnny Snyder, the little eleven-year-old son of Mr. and Mrs. Pearl Snyder, also a victim of lightning in the storm of last Friday, was held from the home of his parents, Sunday afternoon with internment at Midland cemetery.

The three were quiet for a few moments. The only sound was the rhythmic ticking of the grandfather clock in the hallway.

"Poor Graff," said Lucille, breaking the silence. "To lose his wife that way." Ethel just shook her head as tears began to well up in her eyes.

Henry leaned toward her and with a gentle pat on her shoulder said, "Graff will need our prayers." He really didn't know what else to say. The whole thing was so sad and shocking.

"Yes," Ethel agreed. Her heart was breaking as she thought of what her dear childhood friend Graff must be going through.

"I'll be out in the garden..." she heard Henry say softly. His voice trailed off as he walked out through the kitchen to the backyard.

"We must do something for Graff," Ethel said. Lucille nodded in agreement and went back to her chair, picking up some darning she had been working on.

Ethel read the Obituaries again to herself as she quietly wiped tears from her eyes. She then started turning the pages of the newspaper much by habit and glanced at the headlines.

"School Building Tumbling Down—Railroad Time Card"

"Harding Speech of Acceptance—A New Keynote"

"Church Notes—Medical Clinic in Upper Peninsula Wilderness"

Ethel had gotten to page 5 when suddenly she gasped. Lucille immediately looked up from her work, her eyes wide with alarm. "Mama, what's the matter?"

"Oh, no!" was all Ethel could manage to say. Lucille jumped up again and stood near the sofa looking closely at the newspaper. It only took her a second to see a picture of Graff.

"What is his picture doing in there?" Lucille asked, confused. "Is it about the funeral or—"

"No," Ethel interrupted. She raised the paper up to where Lucille could read it.

Announcing Candidacy

Having been much pleased with the support given me in the primaries two years ago by the people of this county, they having given me the second largest number of votes. I take this opportunity of announcing my candidacy on the Republican ticket for the nomination of Sheriff of Midland County in the August primary this year.

Grafton Gawne

"Graff couldn't have known they would print that in this edition. It's unbelievable that the paper..." Ethel was so dumbfounded with the situation that she couldn't put it into words.

Lucille was as shocked as her mother. "We really must do something for Graff."

"Yes," Ethel agreed. "We must think of something to comfort him and lift his spirits. But what?"

She decided she would send a note of sympathy to Graff with her family's deepest condolences. It was the least she could do. She would also write of their desire to see him again, because it had been so long since they had seen each other. If he lived closer, she would have taken food over to the family home. There would no doubt be many visitors at his place. But Graff lived more than fifty miles away. She thought of people that had automobiles that might be willing to drive them there, or they could take the autobus or train, but soon abandoned those ideas. *Where would they stay after they got there?*

Ethel was upset and in tears all day. She fixed the evening meal of roast beef, potatoes, greens, fresh bread, and rhubarb pie. It was delicious as usual, but the family ate in silence after such a joyless day.

Later that evening, Ethel's thoughts drifted back to the days when she and Graff were children growing up as neighbors. She wished she could somehow recapture those happy times. If only she could give the *gift of pleasant memories*, things that can never be taken away. She prayed that God would grant her such a gift for her dear friend.

Chapter 2
Reunited

Written in my hand—Ethel Van Wagnen

Millington, Michigan 1921

Almost eight months have passed since that tragic day in July 1920 when two dear souls were suddenly taken from their loved ones. Methinks that the passing of time alone cannot heal such deep wounds for the ones that have been left behind. But time goes on for all of us to live our lives as it has been appointed.

I begin this book to record what I hope will be happier times for us. We soon shall see what the coming days will bring, and I pray that God will look kindly on us.

On Monday evening, March 14, 1921, shortly after the evening train had arrived from the north, Henry, Lucille, and myself were reading beside the table in the dining room, in this our quiet, humble home. We heard footsteps approaching and upon hearing someone knock at our door, Lucille said, "I'll bet that is Graff."

Henry sprang quickly to his feet and upon opening the door exclaimed, "By Jove, it is Graff! Come in."

He entered the "Old Home" where he was welcomed and made to feel that although it had been years since he had visited us, we were still the same Ethel and Henry whom he had known for many years.

Graff's face looked sad and pale, which his weak smile could not disguise. I thought how much we all wished for happier times for him and decided then and there to do all we could to help him.

Henry led Graff into the parlor and began to catch up on the news while Lucille and I fussed in the kitchen. We prepared a light lunch of hot tea, mince pie, and cold roast beef sandwiches. It gave me great pleasure to serve the luncheon that all seemed to enjoy, especially Graff. We spent the rest of the evening visiting and retired late. Graff stayed in our spare bedroom at the top of the stairs. Lucille prepared his room with some extra quilts and opened the floor vent for some heat. Sleep well, old friend.

Tuesday, March 15, 1921

This is what Lucille looked like on those cold March days.

I told Graff this morning I thought he had forgotten us. He said, "Oh god no, I could never forget."

"Nor could I, Graff." Seeing him again brought to my mind a flood of memories from our childhood, with glimpses of carefree days on our neighboring farms that we must have thought would last forever. Alas, it was not to be.

We had breakfast, and during that time and until 10:00 a.m. we enjoyed visiting. Then I decided to rebuild the kitchen fire and make fried cakes for dinner. I had just enough lard for this batch, but will need to purchase more to have on hand. Later in the afternoon while Graff was up town, I finished frying enough for supper and breakfast tomorrow.

Wednesday, March 16, 1921

We visited until Graff left for Midland on the 10:00 a.m. train, with his promise to come down again in a few weeks. I hope the visit has done him some good and lifted his spirits.

Six weeks later on Sunday, April 24, about 3:00 p.m., Graff drove in from Midland in the old Chevy. Shortly after his arrival, he said, "Let's go for a drive." So, the four of us–Graff, Henry, Lucille, and myself–entered the vehicle and headed south to Otisville, through by Henpeck and then back home. The weather was cool but nice and sunny for our pleasant little trip. Henry was quick to mention the various points of interest along the way.

Here you see Lucille, Graff, Ethel, and Henry

You don't look like the old-time Graff to me, with that moustache on.

Monday, April 25, 1921

When Lucille and Graff insisted on my going out into the backyard early Monday morning for a picture, I did feel as though they could have given me time to comb my hair.

Laddie, if we could only see you smile. Someday we hope to be able to help bring back the old-time smile and luster to those tear-dimmed eyes.

Saturday, May 7, 1921

At 7:30 p.m., Graff drove in bringing my new organ. I had ordered it last month, and it was being sent from Detroit by the evening train. He kindly offered to pick it up from the station and deliver to me. After a little struggle getting it through the front door, the men carefully set it against the east wall of the parlor. It is a beautiful instrument with dark wood and a nice round stool to match. Lucille is very eager to play it. Soon music will be filling every corner of our home.

I see Graff, you decided to shave off your moustache. Good boy, you look better with a clean upper lip.

Sunday, May 8, 1921

We all attended the morning service at the Methodist-Episcopal Church. Reverend Wilson preached on the sacrifice of Jesus, who willingly left the splendor of heaven to come to earth.

And the Word was made flesh and dwelt among us...

After the sermon was completed, Henry and I left our seats in the pew and went forward to join the others in the choir loft. We ended the service with the singing of "Ivory Palaces." It certainly seemed to bless those in attendance, and we were all left with the words of the chorus in our hearts.

"Out of the Ivory Palaces,
Into a world of woe,
Only His great eternal love
Made my Savior go."

After returning home from the service, we went for another pleasant Sunday drive with Graff. Later, we invited our son John and his wife Maybelle, and our daughter Thalia and her husband Vilas and family to come over for supper. My chocolate cake certainly disappeared quickly. Even the grandbabies Theo and Little Billy ate their share.

After all the company made their way back home, Graff invited us to go north fishing with him sometime. *Sounds good to us, we just need to make some plans.* After what seemed to be an enjoyable stay for him, Graff left for home in the evening.

Sunday, May 22, 1921

Two weeks after his last visit, Graff stopped in last evening to spend the night and stay a day or two. Sunday morning, we all got up a little early. I got to work making hot biscuits and chicken gravy. I packed them, fried chicken, sandwiches, cream cake, fruit salad, and cold tea in my lunch basket, and away we went to North Lake. There we spent several hours quietly visiting. I then spread the tablecloth down on a grassy spot, and with Lucille's help put our dinner on the "table." We surely did ample justice to the contents of my basket. Graff said that my biscuits spread with honey just melted in his mouth. Thank-you, dear friend, for the compliment.

Monday, May 23, 1921

There was no washwoman seen around today. Ha ha. We gave up everything as Graff and I lived over again all the pleasant visits and good times we had enjoyed together since early childhood. I was unable to contain my joy at the sight of the old-time smile returning to Graff's face. *I shall always remember this day.*

Sunday, June 5, 1921

Our traveling friend drove in late last evening to stay with us. This morning, I had two well-packed baskets and "our party of four" stepped into the Chevrolet and headed south for Rochester having good roads and only stopping twice.

First stop, Graff was asked to park at a schoolhouse so Henry could jump out and get water for the thirsty engine. Second stop, was when he headed the Chevy into a big hillside to avoid drifting onto a railroad track as the flyer approached the crossing.

We soon reached Rochester and drove into town. We looked down the street and there, standing not a far distance leaning on his cane and talking to a friend was my brother Gene (A.E.) Bailey.

The sad expression on his face soon changed to one of gladness, and he greeted us and made us feel welcome in his little shop "home." Here we visited for an hour.

Then we let Gene get in the front seat with Graff, while Henry, Lucille, and I occupied the backseat. We drove out near the Par Davis farm, where we parked the car. After finding a suitable spot in the grass for our lunch, we spread our tablecloth and unpacked my baskets.

Here you see us just about ready to sit down and eat.

Our dinner consisted of one gallon baked pork and beans, sandwiches, roast beef, fried cakes, cheese, two red raspberry pies, and the four-quart pail of cold tea. Graff had brought a large sack of bananas and oranges. Gene had a large watermelon and two-dozen bananas. Lucille was so proud of us she took the second picture, thinking we might not be able to stand for one after dinner.

It is needless to say we did enjoy our feed, and later when we cut the watermelon, well, all you need to do is to look at us and see if our dinner improved our looks.

And the watermelon—Yum yum!

After spending several hours at this quiet spot, we returned to the Shoe Shop, left our baskets, and took Gene for a nice ride. Then on our return, we lit the oil stove; I made tea and we ate again. At 4:30 p.m., we bade the big boy good-bye and started for home knowing full well how happy we had made him by our visit.

Graff veered off the right road and we drove eight miles in the wrong direction, but oh the beautiful drive.

Let's go again. We certainly enjoyed every mile of the long drive, and it did not seem to bother any of us if the water did keep leaking out of the radiator. Henry was always willing to get out and take the pail and go for more, even if he had to fall down the hillside and go under the bridge to do so. The only trouble was in Graff driving too far sometimes before stopping. Later on, he found to his sorrow; he had let the fan belt run off and from there on he kept having trouble.

At Otisville, we stopped at the home of Cecil and Katie Phipps for a few minutes. Twas good to see Henry's sister for a short visit. Then we went on home, getting there about 8:00 p.m.

We had a cup of hot tea and a light lunch, then at 10:00 p.m., we all retired for the night.

Sunday, June 19, 1921

We all attended the International Order of Odd Fellows memorial service at the IOOF Hall on Park Street, and it was fine. Then we marched to the cemetery, where we all carried flowers and decorated the graves of our brothers and sisters IOOF Rebekahs.

After returning to the hall and leaving our collars, we came home. I hurriedly packed my lunch basket, and we drove ten miles to a pretty spot on the side of the road. We took our basket and pail of tea and crossed the road to the shade of some fine old trees and spread our lunch, which we all enjoyed.

Then we reentered the car and drove to the farm home of Fred and Susan Wildfong living in Thetford. There we found them just doing the evening chores. We visited a few minutes with our dear friends and then came home.

Monday, June 20, 1921

All up at the usual hour. Henry hustled to finish his tax roll and other township supervisor work while I kept out of mischief by doing the housework, making a batch of fried cakes, and baking a white layer cake and Devil's food cake to take with us on our trip.

Late in the afternoon when my jobs were all finished, I asked Graff to back the Chevy out and take me up town. We drove up and stopped in to see Father and Mother Van for a short visit. They were doing well and wished us a fine time on our trip. Then we went on to Wright's Store where we made our final purchases of groceries and what not. Our friend Mr. Wright suggested loaning us his two nice cots to take with us on our trip, which I gladly accepted.

Chapter 3
Setting the Table

Looking Back to the 1880s

The Bailey Farm, Vassar, Michigan
September 1886

Saturday morning was dawning bright and clear as Ethel Bailey shuffled from her bedroom out to the kitchen stove. Mama was already up making coffee and stirring pancake batter in a large, brown bowl.

"Morning," Ethel yawned. Mama looked up from her stirring.

"Good morning, daughter." She smiled. "Sure you're awake?"

Ethel stretched her arms and chuckled. The aroma from the kitchen filled the farmhouse. "Yes, Mama. Mmmm, smells good."

Mama carried the bowl over to the old black skillet and began to scoop out a large spoonful of batter. "Bacon is frying, and I'm about to put the pancakes on. Set the table, dear."

Ethel heard the familiar sound of the batter sizzling as it dropped onto the pan. She went to the shelf and pulled out five large, white plates. Cradling them in her left arm, she pulled the top one off and placed it at the head of the table for her father, John Bailey. "Papa," as she called him, was a hardworking soul, quiet and keeping to himself most of the time. As his youngest child, Ethel held a special place in his heart.

The next plate on Papa's left was for Ella, her older sister. Ella was twenty years old, tall and blessed with dark brown hair and eyes. Ethel adored her sweet-natured sister and secretly yearned to be just like her.

Ethel laid Mama's plate down across from Papa. Lucy Jane Bailey was a short, sturdy woman with energy for hard work. It seemed to Ethel that her mother managed her home with such ease that she would never be able to compare to her. Mama had patience too, which had been tried lately with her youngest daughter.

Ethel stepped around the corner of the table and laid down the plate for her brother, Alfred Eugene. Gene was the name he had gone by since he was a child. He was twenty-two years old now, unmarried and helping his father run the farm. Gene had mentioned to Ethel some time ago that he wouldn't always be a farmer. It seemed he had other plans that might be taking him away someday. If he did leave, Ethel hoped he might only go as far as Vassar, which would only be a few miles from home.

Ethel tried not to think about that as she laid down the last plate for herself at Papa's right hand. It was Ethel who got up during the meal to fetch more of this or that for him. She had just celebrated her thirteenth birthday and was quite content with the way her life was now. Ethel smiled as she thought of her family and the happy memories she had of them living together here on the farm.

Ethel set the knives, forks, and spoons at each plate, along with cups and saucers for her folks' coffee. The children hadn't shown much of an interest in coffee, although Gene drank a cup now and then. Ella and Ethel enjoyed tea when a warm drink was in order, but this morning she would put a pitcher of milk on the table. Ethel would have her usual glass of spring water. She looked in the large wooden bucket sitting on the table by the kitchen door and noticed the water was getting low. That meant she would be making the familiar walk to the spring to fetch some more after breakfast.

Just then, John Bailey stepped out of the bedroom that was off the kitchen, hitching up the shoulder straps on his overalls as he walked. They were well-worn in the knees and faded from many months of hard work in the fields and barn. Ethel greeted him with her usual "Good morning, Papa."

He managed a smile as he said, "Good morning, Lass." Mr. Bailey wasn't much for conversation first thing in the morning, but he never let his sweet daughter know that. Calling her by her pet name was his way of letting Ethel know of his deep affection for her.

Lucy Jane turned from the stove and glanced at her husband. “Pancakes are just about ready,” she announced, knowing that he liked to know how close they were to eating.

John sat down in his chair as Ethel stepped beside him with piping hot coffee and filled his cup near to the brim. She knew her father took it black and would begin to drink it as he waited for the food.

As he began to carefully sip, Ella appeared from the bedroom that she and Ethel shared. She walked slowly toward the kitchen and was secretly glad she wasn’t the last one to the table.

Ella wasn’t an early riser, so the girls had an understanding that she would take care of the breakfast cleanup and wash the dishes. That freed her mother to start on all the daily chores from baking bread, tending the garden, and preparing for the midday and evening meals.

“Good morning, sister,” Ethel practically sung to Ella.

“Morning.” Ella managed to reply, thinking, *How could anyone be so cheerful this early in the day?* She watched Ethel as she moved quickly back and forth from the table to her mother at the stove and she seemed to have everything well in hand. Her younger sister was already much more outgoing and self-assured than she was, and she could picture Ethel’s future life without much struggle for friends, love, and marriage. When the time came, Ethel would most likely end up wedding their neighbor’s boy, Graff. That seemed to be the way things were headed.

She, on the other hand, was at the moment “unattached”, as they say. Ella wondered if her parents were speaking privately about her and concerned about her lack of marriage prospects. She sighed as she slipped into her chair at the table.

Mama placed the last pancake on the stack, which seemed mounded higher than usual. Just then, the familiar sound of footsteps quickly coming down the stairs signaled the arrival of the last family member. Gene hurriedly made his way from his upstairs bedroom, to the table, pulled out his chair and plopped down.

Mr. Bailey gave a quick glance at him and murmured, "Got to get to that plowing first thing, son." Gene nodded as Mama sat down, and Ethel brought the plate of bacon and placed it in front of her father. They all quickly bowed their heads, and after a short prayer by Papa, they began to dig into the meal. Along with the pancakes and bacon, there was also the pitcher of milk, honey, huckleberry jam, butter, and the apple pie left over from last night's supper.

There wasn't much conversation as the family filled their plates, except for the occasional "pass the bacon" or "need some more coffee?" Ethel was enjoying her meal, especially the huckleberry jam that she loved to spread on the warm buttered pancakes. She was very glad her mother had insisted this past summer that the girls go berry picking. The huckleberries were little blue delights, and it was hard to keep from eating them as they picked. Mama wisely canned the jam up quickly before they could disappear.

The breakfast tasted delicious to all the family, but no mention was made regarding it. It seemed this was the usual good food to which they had all become accustomed. She was a wonderful cook and had been passing her skills on to her daughters. They would both need them someday for their own families.

It was hard for Lucy Jane to think about her dear girls gone from their home. Her oldest daughter, Lois ("Ret" as they called her), had been gone since her marriage sixteen years ago when she became Mrs. John Loss. Those days seemed like such a long time ago, and now here she was with more of her children soon to leave the nest.

After everyone had their fill and John had one last big drink of coffee, he pushed his chair back and said, "Let's get going, son. The day's a-wastin'."

Gene shoveled the last piece of pie into his mouth and quickly rose from the table. The two men were up out the door and the women sat for a few minutes sipping their drinks.

Mrs. Bailey, as was her custom, told the girls her plans for the day and what she expected from each of them. Ethel listened carefully to her list of chores, which included peeling and slicing potatoes for supper. Mama had set aside the skillet with bacon grease that would be used to fry them.

Ella was up clearing the table and preparing a kettle of water to heat on the stove for washing dishes. After emptying the bucket of water, Ella handed it to Ethel who took it and without a word headed out the kitchen door. She walked slowly on the path from her home, through the little gate in the fence, swinging the bucket and humming as she walked across the field toward the stream. She glanced up as she passed the clump of maple trees she had played in since she was a child, noticing they were full of soft green leaves bouncing gently in the breeze.

Ethel was feeling happy and so wonderfully blessed when all at once she heard herself say, "This is the day that the Lord hath made. Let us rejoice and be glad in it." She smiled at the sound of the words that seemed to fill her heart with joy.

Soon she reached the creek and the spot where the cold, clear water bubbled out of the bank. Kneeling and tipping the bucket as the sparkling water quickly filled it, she stopped short of the top, knowing how heavy a full bucket would be. She lifted it up and started back to the house struggling a little under the weight that the bucket now held. She would need to make this trip three more times this morning to supply her family their needed water.

This morning's scene with the family breakfast and Ethel's water gathering would happen many times during her childhood years on the farm. As with most daily occurrences, not much was thought of them until later in life when during those quiet moments of reflection, the simple pleasures of a day would come flooding back. The details of a home, the smell of something cooking on the stove, or a look on someone's face would be recalled. A word spoken, or a simple act of love may be carried with someone for a lifetime. Such were the memories of this ordinary day.

Chapter 4
Londo Lake

Millington, Michigan
Tuesday, June 21, 1921

At the Old Home, all ready for the start up north on our fishing trip to Chapman Lake and then on to Londo Lake. Our party consisted of four, all happy and looking forward to a good time.

Henry, Ethel, Graff, and Lucille

Willard took our picture, and immediately after we started on our journey, we headed for Graff's home at Midland. Time of leaving 6:20 a.m. We stopped for five gallons of gas, and then on again along the Tittabawassee riverbanks where green trees and every bush and branch paid silent homage to the water as it rippled and sang along its way. This proved to be the most beautiful part of our long drive.

We reached Midland and the pleasant farm home of our esteemed friend, Grafton Gawne. At 8:40 a.m., we met Mr. and Mrs. Davis (Hod and Amy) who reside there with Graff and help him run the farm.

Shortly after we arrived at the home, Graff took us out to the big barn. Upon reaching the doorway, he pointed out the spot where Lizzie was killed by a bolt of lightning during a severe storm on Friday, July 23, 1920. Then passing along into the cow stable, where he had also found the dead body of little John who had been killed by the same bolt.

We solemnly walked through the barn and allowed Graff to speak of the dreadful events. I don't know how I kept from crying, considering I saw Graff wiping his eyes as we left the stables. *Such a terrible blow it has been to him.*

Then we passed on to the other barns and granary. Graff sent Mr. Davis out to the field and he brought up the racehorses and colt. After some coaxing, Graff and Henry held the horses and got the colt in place, and Lucille took a picture.

Then we started for the house. As we tripped along the path, I discovered a thrashing machine engine standing not too far distance from the barn. I called to the others to come on and get another picture knowing how much Graff would enjoy looking at one. He had for about thirty-five years followed a machine during the fall months of the year.

I climbed hastily to a seat and the others followed me, and this is the result of my happy thought.

We all returned to the house and Lucille called to Mrs. Davis to come out on the front porch and she took her picture.

Then we all went in and prepared for dinner, which we all enjoyed. The potatoes and stewed beef just saved my life, while the others did ample justice to her strawberry shortcake. Henry never thought of leaving the table until he finished his piece of cake, although Mrs. Davis forgot to give us the tea she had ready.

After dinner, we went with Graff and he showed us through his room, looking over books, and keepsakes, etc. Then I prepared medicine for the young lad that helped Graff with the farmwork. He was confined to his bed with poison ivy. Poor fellow.

After Mrs. Davis and the boys finished loading the car and good-byes were said, the driver slowly turned the “Old Chevrolet” around, and we glided out on the highway once more at 12:30 p.m.

Graff says, “Henry, we’ve forgot the stove!” *I thought only women ever forgot*, but we do not turn back.

We came to Edenville and stopped at a store where we bought stamps, postcards, butter, and cheese. Graff returned to the car with bottles of Cherry Tang, “The Best Ever.”

Soon we turned off the main road, and after passing through a long sandy lane, we arrived at the entrance to Chapman Lake. Henry hopped out and let the bars down so we could pass through on down a winding shady road and across a stumpy pasture. On the bank of the babbling brook, we parked the car, and the boys went across the fields and cut poles for stakes to set up our tent. Lucille and I got out of the car, stretched ourselves, and found that we were feeling fine. We looked around for relics but didn't find many. There was not a shady place to sit down in, but the blue-green lake water was quiet and seemed to welcome our party for a restful time.

The boys returned with their poles and quickly set up the tent for our overnight stay. Henry went to the stream for water, built a fire, and we girls soon were ready to serve a hearty meal. Of course, the boys said they were not very hungry but sat down and ate more than we did. After supper, we all gathered our poles and went down to the lakeshore to try our luck. But oh, the fish were such small ones. They were only perhaps six or seven inches long. Lucille got disgusted so we started back for the tent, with Henry and I in the lead. I stopped and picked up a fifty-cent piece off the ground, and Lucille spotted a dime in the grass by the tent. More good luck. Ha ha.

In a short time, Graff and Lucille returned to the lakeshore to try for another catch. I crept away and went out on the bank above the little stream and threw myself face down into the grass. And for the first time in many, many years listened again to the song of the "whip-poor-will."

Henry feared I was lost and called to me several times. I did not answer but lay quietly and alone for some time. When he finally found me, I reluctantly left my grassy refuge, and we returned to the tent to await the others. A little later, Graff and Lucille came back with enough fish for tomorrow's breakfast.

We visited for a short time and then prepared for a night's rest. We all entered the tent and the boys had a soft spot picked out on the ground floor. They spread their heavy blankets and arranged things to their liking and lay down. Lucille and I prepared our beds and with a kind good-night and pleasant dreams said to the boys, we lay down on our comfortable cots. Thanks to our friend Charlie Wright for loaning them to us. They are just fine.

The cows from the nearby farm seemed to realize there are strangers about. So, after Henry had given the mosquitoes their smoky "sleeping potion" and was almost to sleep himself, the cows came along and very meekly tried to peer into the tent. Henry at once took it upon himself to drive them away. But through all the long hours of the night, Lucille could hear the faint tinkle, tinkle of the bells that were around their necks. It seems they liked to wander the fields at night.

Wednesday, June 22, 1921

We are all up and breakfast was ready when I told Lucille to pour the coffee. Our table being somewhat low to the ground, she accidentally put her foot in a cup of hot coffee. I quickly gave her the order to remove her shoe and stocking and as she did so, the skin was also taken off! I hurriedly went to my suitcase and found bandages and ointment and did it up at once. The pain was severe, and even yet methinks I see her sitting beside the tent rocking and crying. Poor girl.

Once breakfast was over, Graff went to the farmhouse of Mr. and Mrs. McGoon to ask for some baking soda. He told Henry he would be back in ten minutes. After waiting fifteen minutes, during which time Henry had been looking at his watch, I started out to meet Graff, or see what the trouble was. I crossed the field and entered the shaded woodland, and in the far distance, I could hear the *tap, tap, tap* of hurried footsteps approaching. Soon I beheld the form of the big lad as he came swiftly down the hillside.

I stepped out and called, "Halt, what's your hurry?"

He only paused long enough to say, "Stay right there," and rushed on. I guess he was afraid that Henry would have the tent taken down and all the work done alone. He certainly was in a hurry.

All things were in readiness for leaving Chapman Lake, and at 9:40 a.m., we were again on our way, only stopping at the farmhouse long enough to return the pail we borrowed. Then on we went, reaching West Branch at 10:20 a.m. The boys got out, and Henry bought ice cream cones. After enjoying them, we saw a doctor crossing the street, and as he passed close to us, I inquired of where to find my cousin Lura Smith. With his kindly way, he gave us the directions.

Graff drove to the corner and could go no farther on account of a big crew of men working on the street. When we arrived at Lura's house, Henry got out and went to the door, but she was gone. He took her *Detroit Journal* from the door and returned to us and on we went again leaving West Branch at 10:45 a.m.

A few miles farther on, we stopped at a little store. Henry went in to buy cookies as another car drove up and halted for a few minutes. The boys learned that they are also going to Londo Lake so Graff let them take the lead, and we followed the Detroit car the rest of the way.

"Look out, Graff! Close call, you almost hit their rear end. Drive slower, old boy."

Landed at Londo Lake
Wednesday, June 22, 1921

We were welcomed by E.T. Pedlow of Millington and Burt Clark of Vassar. Ed says, "Pitch your tent right here." Graff ran the car around and faced it toward the lake. Ed stayed and helped put the tent up. They called me to help and someone let a pole fall and it hit me on the head and knocked me down. I refused to help anymore and went outside to watch. Finally, the tent was up and secured so we started to unload our belongings. Ed advised Graff to rent a boat at once. He went to the farmhouse on the hill and all boats were gone except their own, so the lady rented him that one.

Our four took turns going out in the boat fishing and soon had a nice bunch. Here you see us posing with our first catch of pike.

This little path led one through the barbed wire fence to a quiet spot called "The Cedars." Lucille caught the big laddie as he was about to step through the fence. In his right hand, he brought a tall branch of asparagus to me, and he placed it across my lap. The kindly look and pleasant smile you see upon his face nearly always lingered there during those happy days at Londo Lake.

Back at camp, Graff raked our "backyard" and Henry came up with a bundle of straw for their bed. In a short time, all but myself were quietly sleeping. I detected the smell of smoke and aroused Henry. He quickly went out on "dress parade" and put the campfire out.

Henry often took the dishpan and went to the lake for dishwater. Lucille would say, "Be careful, Papa, don't spill a drop." See one of our boats anchored at the landing in this picture.

Thursday, June 23, 1921 at 5:00 a.m.

Our boys dressed quietly and went out on the lake. Shortly after, E.T. Pedlow passed our tent on his way to the lake. He called out, "Time you ladies were getting up!"

And true to the word, we threw off our light coverings and bound out. Our boys got one pike, but E.T. came back empty-handed. We all went up to the Pedlow tent for a visit.

Lucille brought along the Kodak and got some pictures. Here you see left to right: Bert Clark, Grafton Gawne, and E.T. Pedlow. Three husky fishermen standing beside the Pedlow car, with Bert nursing a sore finger from a fish hook.

A little later, just as Mrs. Pedlow was washing dishes and Mrs. Clark was ready to spread a sandwich, Lucille caught them.

The Pedlows left for home at 9:00 a.m., taking our Millington letters home with them. Later we learned that for some reason, Ed ran into the ditch. No one was hurt, but it awakened Mrs. Pedlow from a sound sleep.

We returned to our tent and started breakfast, leaving Henry to watch the fish we had frying. He stayed right on the job until it was done and then helped eat it. I cut the "Devil's Food Cake" and it was fine.

Graff said, "Ethel, when we come again, don't bother to bake any other kind of cake. This is good enough."

"Thank you," I replied. Just let me mention Graff's ham, which I had boiled and it was good. It seemed everything tasted better on this trip in the outdoors.

After breakfast, Graff went to the farmhouse on the hill and rented another boat. Henry took Lucille in the blue boat while Graff and I boarded the brown one, and away we went.

The fish seemed to be elsewhere this morning, and I refused to go back empty-handed. So, my companion rowed around and guided the boat into a quiet, little shady cove. There we found what looked to be a delicate floating garden. Graff paused the boat and let me gather a large bouquet of beautiful water lilies. I looked down upon their snow-white petals and with a lingering touch gently gathered them into my arms. I felt it was far better to have the privilege of enjoying my flowers now than to wait and in later years have them laid upon my casket.

Surely the Good Lord was looking down and reminding us:

> *Consider the lilies how they grow: they toil not, they spin not; and yet I say unto you, that Solomon in all his glory was not arrayed like one of these.*

When we arrived back at camp, Henry was standing at the landing to meet us. Later, Lucille caught her father sitting on a stump upon the hill in back of the tent.

Hurry Graff, here is one more to clean.

Graff and Lucille went up to the farmhouse for potatoes, which we were waiting to cook for dinner. Upon leaving home, Graff had placed his pocketbook in my hand and said, "Take care of this for me." So today he came to me and said, "Give me five cents please."

"What for?"

He said, "Potatoes are ten cents per bushel up here, and I just brought down half a bushel."

Well, as long as he was not going to spend his money foolishly, I gave it to him. Ha ha.

Henry and I pared potatoes for dinner, fried bacon, made lemonade, and put dinner on the table. Everybody was hungry and able to do ample justice to everything we set before them.

After dinner, Graff said, "If you ladies will powder and fix up a little, we will all drive over to Hale and get a few supplies."

We at once made our *toilet* and got freshened up. He went out to the car and found to his discomfort that he had forgotten to turn the switch off yesterday, and now his battery was all run down. He came back to the tent looking sober and said, "We don't want to go to Hale today, for we don't care to walk."

Lucille and I felt we had wasted a lot of powder all for nothing. She got her fancy work out, stepped outside the tent, and went to work on her embroidering. I took my book, *The Island of Regeneration,* and quietly stepped into the car. I adjusted the cushions to fill my head and back and then settled down.

Later on, we all decided to go out on the lake for more fishing, and I caught two big pike. Lucille got two nice ones too, and when the boys decided they had tried long enough, we all went back to the tent.

Lucille and Graff got supper ready as Henry built the fire. Someone always reminds him, *"Don't cut your hand with that butcher knife."*

Friday, June 24, 1921

After a refreshing night's rest, we were once more ready for the lake. At 5:30 a.m., Henry and I led out and the other two followed. We had good luck and returned to camp at 8:00 a.m.

Graff built a fire, and we fried fish, boiled potatoes, made coffee, and enjoyed a good breakfast. Afterwards, we visited for a while, and then Henry slipped away and got his book, *The Chip of the Flying,* and seated himself beside his favorite tree to read. After a while, we were all sleepy, except the big laddie, and we lay down and were almost asleep when he came marching in with a young robin. I got up and fed it. Then we all went out and up the hillside for a walk. I found a glass vinegar cruet, which I held in my right hand while Lucille said, "Line up and I'll take your picture while that dreamy look is still there."

She got it all right.

Chapter 5
Stricken

Looking Back to the 1880s

The Bailey Home—February 1887

Thirteen-year-old Ethel Bailey struggled with the bucket of ice-cold water she had just drawn from the spring some distance from her home. Even though the little creek was frozen over, the spring was still flowing for now. She was making her way through more than a foot of snow, and now the wind was picking up as it blew fine snow, stinging her face and swirled around the drifting pathway.

Ethel felt hot, achy, and chilled all at the same time. She knew she was "coming down with something" but needed to press on. She was feeling worse by the minute and wondered if she would make it through the snow without dropping the bucket. Her feet were numb from the cold, and her shoes were wet clear through. The water in the wooden bucket sloshed more than usual under her trembling hands.

Finally, she reached the kitchen door and entered the house. She lifted the bucket and placed it on the table by the kitchen stove. Mama stood by the stove stirring some soup and looked up just as Ethel collapsed on the floor. Rushing to her side, she lifted her daughter up to sit and touched her face. "Why, you're burning up with fever, child!"

She managed to raise Ethel up and walk her to the girls' bedroom, then quickly laid her on the bed while pulling off her coat, scarves, and mittens. Her legs were hanging off the bed, so she decided to leave Ethel's shoes on for now and just quickly covered her with a quilt before rushing to the kitchen door. She stepped outside and gave a loud yell for help, knowing her older daughter Ella was nearby in the chicken coop and her husband was probably in the barn. One of them would hear her and be there any minute, so she dashed back into the house. By the time she had gotten Ethel's shoes and stockings off, she heard Ella coming in.

"What's wrong, Mama?" Ella said breathlessly as she entered the bedroom doorway. Seeing her younger sister on the bed, she knew at once this was serious.

"Help me get her clothes off and get her into bed."

Ella at once did as her mother said. Ethel was not much help, and she moaned in pain as they dressed her in a warm nightgown. Soon she was tucked into bed, and Mama said to Ella, "She's got a bad fever. Gather some of your things and take them into my bedroom. We will share a bed and Papa will move into Gene's room to sleep."

Mama filled a basin with water and began applying cold cloths to Ethel's forehead. The rest of the family fell into the new arrangement quickly, and Ella took over many of Mama's duties so she could keep vigil over Ethel, applying the cold cloths and offering her weak tea and broth.

But Ethel refused to eat much of anything since her throat was so sore she could hardly swallow. Gene would scoop small bowls of snow and bring them into Ethel. She would manage a few spoonsful to cool her burning throat but was soon suffering again. Mama sat in a chair by Ethel's bed during the day and lay across the end of her bed that night. She wanted to be close to her and would wake throughout the night to care for her and keep the fire going in the stove. This would continue to be her routine for many days. Ethel was in and out of sleep and lost track of time or what day it was.

After languishing for several days, Ethel showed no signs of improvement. Mama was very worried, so she sent Gene into town in the buggy to fetch Dr. Miller. Within the hour, the doctor arrived at the Baileys. He entered Ethel's room, sat on the chair next to the bed, and spoke to her in his deep voice.

"Now, young lady, what seems to be your problem?"

Gene had already informed Dr. Miller about Ethel on their way to the Baileys, so he had an idea what was ailing her.

Ethel answered in barely a whisper, "Oh, Doctor, I have never been so sick."

Dr. Miller felt Ethel's face and under her jaw for swelling. He checked her with his stethoscope as Mama filled him in with the other symptoms besides the sore throat and fever. There was a rash (which he had already noticed), pains in her stomach, and every joint in her body seemed sore to touch. Dr. Miller directed Ethel to open her mouth as wide as she could and he took a look. He then placed a thermometer under Ethel's tongue as he listened to Mama describe her daughter's misery during the bad fever sessions.

Ethel lay quietly and looked closely at Dr. Miller's face with his well-tended beard and mustache. After removing the thermometer, Dr. Miller squinted and read it but made no mention of it as he put it away. He finished his visit with a little smile to Ethel, and after reaching in his bag, he placed some hard candy in her hand. He stood and told her that he would stop by again in a few days. Ethel looked in her hand and saw several lemon drops. She weakly placed one in her mouth and savored the tart flavor as she rested back on her pillow.

At the door, Dr. Miller told Mrs. Bailey he suspected Ethel had scarlet fever, and there wasn't much to be done except continue her care. As the doctor left to get into the buggy, Mama saw the neighbor boy, Grafton Gawne, walking across the barnyard toward the house.

Graff was a welcomed sight and as dear to Mr. and Mrs. Bailey as if he were their own son. He was soon to be seventeen years old and such a good friend of the family, especially Ethel. Graff stepped into the house and stood by the door and spoke with Mrs. Bailey inquiring how Ethel was doing. She told him what the doctor said and Graff asked if he could do anything to help.

Mama decided to try a remedy that she had used in the past. She sent Graff to get some willow tree bark, which she would boil and make into a tonic to fight the fever. Her poor girl had been nearly out of her head at times from the fever.

Graff was very worried about Ethel and came every day to see how she was feeling. He helped the family by fetching water from the spring and chopping wood. Mama's "tonic" seemed to help with the fever some, after she began adding a bit of honey for Ethel to get it down.

Ella had been needed for extra help in the kitchen since Mama was nearly exhausted from caring for Ethel day and night. Many times, she found herself praying by her daughter's bedside for God to spare her life. As her tears flowed, so did the petitions to her heavenly Father.

At the next visit from Dr. Miller, Mama met him at the door, took his coat and hat, and held them as she told him how Ethel had fared the past few days. Even though she still had a fever, her tonic seemed to bring it down. Dr. Miller nodded his approval and walked into Ethel's bedroom to find her sitting up in bed to greet him.

"Hello, Dr. Miller," she said in the cheeriest voice she could manage.

He smiled and asked, "Well, now how is my favorite patient doing?"

"Better, I think," she replied.

Mama stood at the doorway and watched as the doctor checked Ethel's throat and placed the thermometer in her mouth, before opening his black bag and pulling out his stethoscope. He began to listen intently to her heart and lungs, asking her to breathe deeply, while stopping and listening in one particular spot for some time. He pulled the stethoscope from his ears and took Ethel's hand and pressed his fingers to her thin wrist. The room was quite still as he waited for a time. Then he gently placed her hand back on the bed and covered it with the quilt. He removed the thermometer, and as before, did not mention anything about it. Mama gripped the doctor's coat in fear as she waited for him to speak.

He finally looked at her and said, "Keep up with the cold cloths and tonic for the fever. She is still too weak to be getting out of bed." Dr. Miller noticed the look of concern on Mama's face and added, "She should be coming out of this soon. I believe the worst is over."

Mama was relieved to hear that and looked at Ethel who seemed glad to hear that news, too. She managed a little smile as the doctor packed up his bag and told her to mind what her Mama told her.

"I will," Ethel responded weakly. Before heading out of the room, he held out his closed hand to Ethel. She raised her hand, and he deposited some lemon drops, which she eagerly received. "Thank you." she said.

Mama walked to the door and handed Dr. Miller his coat and hat. After putting them on, he turned to her and lowered his voice. "Mrs. Bailey, Ethel has rheumatic fever, and her condition is more serious than I first thought. She is recovering, but we may not know for some time whether her heart has been damaged permanently. I'll be back on Saturday to check on her."

And with that, he was gone. Her own heart sank, as the words from the doctor seem to hang in the air. She stood there staring at the door and fighting back the tears, deciding she would not tell Ethel of this news for now. Her daughter needed to get well, and knowing this would not help her.

"Mama," she heard Ethel call. She took a deep breath, turned, and headed back to the bedroom.

The next few days turned out better for Ethel. The fever had finally left her for good, and she was eating a little better. Mama had returned to her own bedroom to sleep and resumed most of her other household duties. Still, Ethel was weak and confined to her bed, which she was feeling very weary of. She longed to get up and go outside for some fresh air, even though it was "freezing out" as Ella complained each time she left the warm house. Still, *Anything would be better than these four walls*, she thought.

Every day, Papa and Gene would lean their heads into her room to say "hello" before heading out to their chores. Ella visited with her sometimes when she had a few moments to spare. She would stand at the bedroom doorway and tell Ethel of the latest happenings she could think of. It usually included stories and well wishes from their nearby neighbors at the Gawne farm.

Once in a while, Ethel would see little chickadees land outside her window. They would chirp and hop around on the snow-covered branches for a few minutes, and then they were gone. They were such friendly little birds; she wished she could entice one to come in and perch on her finger.

Ethel was feeling up to reading for a while, so some books, including the family Bible, were brought to her bed. She had missed several weeks of school and worried that she might get too far behind the others. Her teacher, Miss Johnson, had sent word to her not to worry. She said that Ethel was a bright student, and she would help her to catch up when she returned.

One day, Mama came into Ethel's room with a basket full of yarn, thread, needles, and what not.

"I think you are up to some crocheting and embroidering," Mama said with a smile. Ethel took the basket and looked inside, eager to get started. She thought about making a nice large dresser scarf but decided she would start with crocheting a small doily. Mama had taught her the basics, so it was just a matter of getting started. "Call me if you need any help," Mama said as she left to go to the kitchen.

As Ethel began to sort through the basket, she glanced in the corner of the bedroom at her cedar chest. She called it her "Hope Chest," because along with various household items she was beginning to collect, it held her hopes for marriage and the promise of love and security. Ethel's mind danced with the dreams of marrying, having babies, and caring for a home someday.

She loved the pleasant scent of the chest when she would open it to place something inside or just look over the contents. Papa had told her that the cedar wood kept moths and such away. It was comforting to know that her treasures were safe and snug there until the day she would finally pull them out to use in her very own home.

With these thoughts in her mind, Ethel began her work on the doily. It would be one of many she would finish as she kept herself busy with her needlework throughout the long days she was confined to her "sick-bed." Little did she realize that down through the years, they would be a cherished reminder of her young life spent on the farm and of her dreadful illness.

All during the time Ethel was convalescing, Graff was still fetching water for the family every day. One morning, he came to the door to see how Ethel was doing. Mrs. Bailey invited him in to see for himself. He timidly walked to her bedroom doorway and saw her sitting up in bed with her covers drawn up to her neck. He noticed how pale and thin she looked but smiled at her just the same as he always did.

"Laddie!" Ethel called to him. Graff secretly loved the name that the Bailey family had bestowed upon him.

"I have something for you, Ethel." He handed her two small parcels that were wrapped in newspaper. She excitedly opened the first one, which was a block of cheese. "That's from the children. They wanted you to eat it and get well," Graff said softly.

Ethel was so surprised at the thoughtfulness of this gift. It meant so much coming from Graff's brothers and sisters. She knew it was no small sacrifice to part with food that would have helped feed their large family.

"Oh, please tell them thank you so much," Ethel said sincerely. Graff nodded and smiled. "Mama, may I have a little piece with some tea and biscuits?" Mrs. Bailey happily agreed and went to put the kettle on.

Ethel opened the next package, and inside was a little wooden cross the size of her hand. She looked at it closely and realized that it had been carved for her. On the back were written the words, "I am the God that heals thee," and at the bottom, Graff had signed his name.

Ethel hugged the cross and thanked Graff for the beautiful gift. He decided he had stayed long enough and took his leave, feeling that it had been a good visit. Ethel thought the same and treasured the cross that she knew had been given to her with love.

Several days later, Ethel woke up early as the sun was rising. She slowly sat up and felt she was strong enough to get to her feet. Pulling the covers back, she swung her legs around to the side of the bed. She waited to see how she felt and decided after a minute that she could manage by herself. It felt cool out from under the covers, but at least that wretched fever and sore throat were gone. For that, she was thankful and had told the Good Lord so many times.

She slowly stood up beside her bed, knowing that in case she felt weak, she could plop back down and no one would be the wiser. She could feel that her long illness had taken much of her strength, but she was determined to get up and "back with the living."

Turning to the high-backed chair next to her bed, she pulled the heavy wool shawl off the back and wrapped it around her shoulders. The house seemed very chilly, and Ethel guessed the fire was probably out. She decided she would tend to it and surprise her family with a warm house when they awoke.

Shuddering as she walked across the cold floor on her bare feet, she slowly and carefully made her way to the kitchen. Opening the door on the stove, she saw it was down to a few orange coals, so she took several small pieces of kindling from the wood box and laid them on the coals. She pulled the door almost shut, leaving a small gap to get the fire going. Soon she heard the crackling noise from inside and reached for a bit larger piece of wood.

I wonder if Graff split this, she thought as she added it to the fire. This time, she closed the door and stood by the stove as it slowly began to warm the room. Feeling quite weak from her excursion, she decided to pull up a chair and rest by the fire. It wasn't long before she heard a voice from behind her. "My sakes, what are you doing out of bed?"

It was Mama, with such a surprised look on her face. She quickly made her way to Ethel and wrapped her arms around her, holding her there for a blessed moment before releasing her.

"You should be in bed, dear," Mama scolded in the most unconvincing tone.

Ethel just smiled at her and said, "Someone had to get some heat into this house!" They both laughed, and what a relief it was after so many weeks of distress.

"I'm hungry," announced Ethel. She didn't say it expecting Mama to wait on her. She just wanted to let her dear mother know she was feeling better and getting back to her old self.

She stayed in the chair while Mama began to make breakfast for the whole family. She was so happy to be out of that bed that she didn't fuss about helping just now, knowing it wouldn't be long before she would be back at her regular chores, returning to school, and quite ready for a certain neighbor to visit.

Ethel did not know then that she had not entirely escaped the harm done by her illness. True, God had spared her life, but she had received some damage to her heart. It would be weaker now, and she would, at times throughout her life, be stricken with the effects of the rheumatic fever. There would be bouts of weakness in her heart, severe headaches, and general failing health.

But for now, her heart was light and grateful for God's healing touch and for the loving care of her mother. For here she was, ready to have breakfast as before, with the ones she loved so dearly.

Chapter 6
Londo Lake—We Continue

Friday, June 24, 1921, 11:00 a.m.

We continued with our Londo Lake camping trip on this pleasant day when a gentleman and his two nephews, all from Flint, came down from the hill above us with their Ford sedan. They connected wires to the Chevrolet and charged the battery and would only accept our thanks for their kindly assistance.

Shortly after, our boys started for Hale. As they did, Graff broke the reverse lever and Henry ran back to tell us they will come back for us in a short time. But instead of buying a new one, (which could not be found in Hale), and rather than drive to Whitmore, a distance of twelve miles, Graff said he could make one. Which he did, and at 2:30 p.m., they returned.

Yesterday morning before leaving for home, Mrs. Clark asked one of our party if Graff was Henry's boy. Needless to say, Graff was so pleased he said he would like to buy her a new dress, but instead Lucille and I caught him standing on his head.

"Big Lad"

At 3:00 p.m., we had dinner and watched a thunderstorm approaching. We lay down to rest, but the storm soon broke and as the rain fell heavily, our tent leaked in some places. Henry and Graff were fussing around, hoping their bed wouldn't get wet. The thunder, lightning, and rain continued, wetting up the straw in the boys' bed.

At 5:20 p.m., we all prepared for the lake again. Lucille and Henry got out on the lake ahead of us. Graff was hunting for hooks and line that had been misplaced and couldn't find them. "*Remember, it wasn't Graff's fault.*" Ha ha.

Lucille got a perch and I got a nice large bass, but the big laddie had to help me. We surely thought we had a whale, and he had our line all tied up in a knot by the time we got him in the boat.

As the wind was in the east, the fishing was poor today. Lucille and Henry got discouraged and went up first, and soon after, we followed them. They had a hot supper ready of boiled potatoes with their jackets on, fried bacon, cold fish, fresh bread, lovely butter, and tea. Everything tasted good, too.

We decided not to stay up very long, as it was cold and damp. Evening gowns were brought forth, also union suits and sweaters to keep us warm and comfortable. Good-nights were then said and all retired.

Saturday, June 25, 1921

After a good night's rest, we were all up and feeling fine. Henry built the fire, Graff and I made the beds, while Lucille washed last night's dishes. Graff started to clean the fish and discovered he had lost his ring. I went down to the lake and found it in the boat. He said, "Good girl."

Breakfast menu: Hot coffee, bread, butter, fried fish, and dry fried cakes.

At 9:00 a.m., our Flint friends were pulling up stakes and preparing to leave. Graff went up to see them, and they sent him back to ask me for a safety pin, which I gladly furnished for the fellow that had ripped "something."

Our boys came up on the hill and found me reading my book. Henry put his hat on my head, and they sat down beside me. Lucille sprang up from her blanket on the grass and said, "Look pleasant, please." We tried to.

At 9:40 a.m., we left for Hale to get the mail. There was a rough road around the corner and also lots of sand. We traveled along and came upon a large Robbins Overland Show Co. sign with a picture of a red-headed girl in a risqué, blue dress. Graff was so taken by her, he almost stalled his car. We all had a good laugh over that.

We arrived at Hale at 10:10 a.m. The car was parked near the corner, and Henry went into the post office. He was told the mail train was running one hour late.

Graff said, "Ethel, we'll wait for the train for you may get word from home."

Soon we heard a band playing. Lucille, still unable to wear her shoe on her burned foot, got out of the car and hobbled along to the corner where she sat herself on a stone and listened to the music. Henry walked to the depot to wait for the train but amused himself by fooling two pretty girls who were pitching pennies by telling them the train was coming and they would have to hurry. They picked up their suitcases and rushed out to find it was the section men on the handcar.

Graff fixed the fan belt on his car, and we headed to the Hale Oil station to buy two gallons of gas, where we paid 21¢ per gallon. As we waited for the slow train, they were picking on me and my gabardines. "Hands off please."

At 12:18 p.m., the train finally arrived. Henry went to the post office and soon returned bringing me a nice long letter from daughter Thalia and a postcard from dear old mother Van saying all is well at home. Graff said, "That was worth waiting for."

Away we went back to Londo Lake and reached our tent at 12:45 p.m. Everybody was hungry so we hurried and ate dinner, then cleared our table. Henry tried to shave but only got the whiskers off one side and quit. No wonder the boat was lopsided. Ha ha.

Henry and I went out fishing, and he caught twenty-two bluegills while I only got a couple. While he was putting the last fish in the pail, he said to me, "I did not think I was going to enjoy myself up here, but *By Jove*, I'm having a good time." Tis good to hear him say so.

This afternoon, as I took a quiet walk out in the Cedars, I noticed a piece of newspaper on the ground. I picked it up and one of the items read: "Willard Van Wagnen spent Tuesday in Columbiaville." Whoever would have thought *The Millington Herald* would blow as far north as Londo Lake?

This is the way these two great big kiddies looked most of the time while we were fishing.

Lucille

I'm sure if anyone could get a picture of Lucille any time during the night, she would look a lot different. For just across the road from our tent was a cluster of trees where every night the cows assembled and stood guard over us. We could hear the music of their bells during all the long night. Somehow, Lucille did not enjoy it.

In this next picture, away back in the distance you can see "The Island."

Graff—Waiting

You do look awful dark in this picture, Laddie Boy, but it is not because you feel out of sorts for any reason. For I can honestly say that you have never given me a cross look or unkind word in your life.

I have enjoyed all the creatures here at Londo Lake. Today, the old cat from the farmhouse caught one of our busy little chipmunks and carried it away. Mean old thing. I have heard the frogs as one by one each joined in the evening chorus, and I always listened and loved to hear the deep-toned notes of the bass.

The Sabbath Day-Sunday, June 26, 1921

Remember the Sabbath day to keep it holy.

When we planned our trip and knew we would remain from our home over Sunday, it was mutually agreed by all members of our little party that we would not do any fishing. Instead, we planned to take our lunch and drive quietly across the plains and view the Au Sable River power dams and "High Rollway."

At 8:30 a.m., we had our breakfast and were ready for our drive to the Big Dams. We drove up the hill, and Henry went to the farmhouse and soon returned and said, "I just found E.S. Bankert, and Will Lowell of Millington had just driven in ahead of me." The homeboys came out, and we welcomed them to our pleasant little spot near Londo Lake, which I had rightly named "Look Out Cottage."

We picked up Stanley French beyond Hale, and he came with us as our guide. Soon we passed National Forest Boundary Line and saw some beautiful red lilies.

At 10:35 a.m., Graff parked the car on a hill that led to Big Dam. We all got out of the car, went down the hill, and stopped on the big bridge. Lucille and I did not wear our hats, and the sun was blistering hot. I took the *Detroit Journal*, which Henry had taken from Lura's doorway at West Branch and had been left in the car. I gave half of it to Lucille, and we used it as sun bonnets to protect our faces from the hot sun. We crossed the bridge after Lucille had taken this picture of the powerhouse and dam.

We all stood at the right, and where you see the reflection of the powerhouse in the water, Graff counted fourteen large pickerel. They seemed to know we could not harm them, and they rested and enjoyed themselves in the warmth of the sun.

I left the others and went back to the bridge and let myself down step by step from log to log several feet below where I sat down on the end of a huge timber and rested in the shade.

After spending a little time there, we returned to our car and started for the High Rollway. Graff parked the car, and we all descended the long, steep hill 260 feet below to drink from a cold spring, which trickled and ran along. This place was only partly shadowed by the heavy foliage from the overhanging boughs, while here and there the sparkling sunlight brightened the way.

We crept along, then we all stepped from beneath the branches of the trees and stood on the riverbank. Graff and I went out upon some logs to rest awhile and enjoyed the view of the quiet river floating along past the high bank. Then we started on the long uphill climb, which I found pretty tiresome. Henry offered his assistance, but I was "game" and reached the top unaided.

Here we are at the top of the hill at last. We all went to the car where we meet the folks from Hale, Standish, and some from Flint. Lucille and

I spread out the lunch I had prepared. The cold tea just hit the spot. After everyone has satisfied their hunger, we proceed to the High Rollway where Lucille took this picture.

From this point, we all tried to throw stones far enough to hit the water below, but even the big husky boys failed to hear the water splash. That done, we returned to the car and started across the plains once more.

On we went and arrived at South Branch at 2:20 p.m. Graff parked the car in front of the store on Main Street. I got out and crossed the street to the South Branch Post Office to find my cousin Addie Martindale, who is the postmistress. I found the doors closed, and a lady next door told me we could find them a half mile west of town where a new house is being built. I went back to the car and reported.

Graff said, “Get in and we'll drive down there.” He is a good old sport.

We arrived and found the girls just eating dinner. After a hearty greeting, Lucille took our picture. I tried to keep as far in the background as possible, giving my two sweet-faced cousins a good front view.

After a pleasant visit catching up with all the family news, we started on our journey back to Londo Lake. We soon passed Loon Lake and Graff remarked, “This is great pastureland. I never saw better.”

We arrived back at Look Out Cottage where all is okay. We noticed that our friends Bankert and Lowell had their tent set up, and everything was in fine shape. They were out on the lake fishing.

We built a fire and cooked a good warm supper. Lucille and I took our books and went out in the car to read. The boys were enjoying each other’s company somewhere.

Sunday evening at 6:30 p.m., a messenger drove up beside us, having driven from Whitmore with a telegram for E. E. Bankert.

Henry jumped into action and said, “I’ll take our boat and go and bring him in.” Lucille went with him.

Graff and I went into the tent, and I was feeling somewhat nervous fearing the telegram might mean bad news for us. Graff stared at me. “Ethel, go over and sit down on that cot. You’re as white as a sheet.”

Later, on Bankert’s arrival, we all felt relieved that while the telegram called him home at once to attend to funerals, it did not bring sadness into any of our lives in a personal way.

Lucille and I went up to their tent and prepared a supper for them while they tore down their tent and packed up. Poor fellows, they had driven from Millington since midnight and only had the pleasure of catching one small fish apiece and had to start on the long journey back home. "Tis too bad."

We stood by and watched them until all was in readiness and then with a warm handclasp bid them a kind good-bye. They moved out from beneath the overhanging boughs of the trees, and soon we knew the little white house upon the hill was hidden from their view.

Monday, June 27, 1921

All up and out on the lake at 5:30 a.m., Henry and Lucille went out to the left of the landing, while Graff and I went to the right. I called to her that I would try for the first catch; but she beat me, getting three nice ones while we came up later without any.

At 8:30 a.m., Graff and I went up, built a fire, and fixed up cots as Henry cleaned the fish. Lucille made coffee, and we soon all had breakfast.

The boys spent the morning resting and visiting while Lucille and I spread a blanket in the shade of a large maple tree and read our books.

Later, Graff went across to South Londo Lake and returned with a basin of nice red raspberries, which he placed in my lap.

"Thank you, Laddie. We will enjoy them for dinner, which I'm going to get to in a few minutes."

Graff then went into the tent to wash up and was very liberal with the salt. He rubbed his face and hands with it, thinking he had gotten into poison ivy. After dinner, we went out "still fishing" and Henry had good luck. Graff and Lucille followed us in, and I discovered Graff's forehead was nearly blistered, the result of s*alt and sunshine.*

Later, when Graff and I went out trolling, a storm threatened and Henry was afraid I would be tipped over and drowned. But the big lad said, "I won't run any risk. If the wind begins to blow, I'll row to the nearest landing, cast anchor, and we'll walk up."

The storm held off and I got two large pike but lost our best line and "Wahjack" after getting a big pike within arm's length of the boat.

Graff said, "Ethel, I'd love to stay another week, but Henry thinks he must go home tomorrow, so we will go. For some of the Millington folks thought I couldn't keep him up here over three or four days, and we've been here a week. So I'll go home satisfied."

We then went back up to camp and found Lucille had a nice hot supper ready for us. This was our last evening in our cozy "cottage," and we spent it visiting and singing by the fire. Just before supper, I moved the big table into the tent with Graff's help, and we prepared for rain which began at 9:30 p.m.

At 10:30 p.m., the big laddie decided he would run down to the lake and take a bath. But after coming out of the warm water, he was suddenly chilled. He came hurriedly back to the tent wrapped in his blanket with teeth chattering loud enough to disturb our peaceful slumber.

After a gentle rub down to start circulation, we heard him creep in beside Henry. Then, after the straw and a few feathers had been smoothed out to his liking, he quietly drew the warm blankets up over him and went to sleep.

But, for some reason or other, both boys were restless and from time to time we heard them as they tossed from first one side to the other. Quite frequently, they reached out for the few stray mosquitoes that seemed to take delight in getting into that particular corner. I thought it was because the storm was over and the moon had come up, but later I discovered it was Henry's bald head that had attracted their attention. Then I loaned him my large piece of mosquito netting, which had been folded and carefully placed in my suitcase before leaving home. Graff discovered a little "whiff" in the cottage, but thought it was best not to say anything about that. Ha ha.

Tuesday, June 28, 1921

We are all up at 5:30 a.m. Graff and I went out on the lake trolling for the last time, leaving Lucille and Henry to pack up and then get the breakfast. We got two nice pike and finally came up hungry enough to eat all that Lucille had cooked.

After breakfast, Graff went up to the farmhouse on the hill to pay his last bill. At 10:30 a.m., Lucille took this picture of our little tent home, See All Cottage, where we had spent so many pleasant hours during our stay at Londo Lake.

Lucille and Henry loosened the ropes down, folded the tent up, and it was ready to pack. All that was left to show we were there was the matted grass, where the boys slept, and the ashes of our cozy campfire.

Graff ran the Chevrolet up the hill to pump up the tires and sees that all is in readiness for the long drive home. Lucille told me I would have to ride in the front seat as she is going to sit behind with Papa. So I went up and told Graff, "I've been ordered to ride in the front seat."

He smiled and said, "All right, that's just where I want you."

At 10:55 a.m., I took my place beside our friend for the first time since leaving home. Henry walked up beside the car and Graff says, "Strike her off, Henry, and we will be on our way."

Henry stepped to the front of the machine, bent down, and firmly grasped the lever. Then with one strong, quick pull, the motor began to chug. With a look of satisfaction, he came back and got in beside Lucille. We all took one glance backward and bid a fond farewell to Londo Lake. Up the drive we went, past the farmhouse on the hill that sits so peacefully waiting for our return someday.

We reached Hale and parked the car by the grocery store. I went in and purchased bologna, cookies, butter, and so forth. While there, I heard dreadful news of a double murder at Tawas. I returned to the car, and we drove to an oil station to buy three gallons of gas. Away we went and left Hale at 11:30 a.m.

We soon passed a nice field of potatoes. Graff turned his head to the backseat and said, "Henry, these are the best potatoes we've seen yet." Henry agreed.

Upon his request, I put a cushion behind the driver's back. Henry noticed and announced, "I'm sitting on mine." Ha ha. *Watch those bumps, Laddie.*

We traveled on passing through the little towns of Whitmore, Twining, and then Omer, where we made a short stop for Henry to get some water for the machine. It seemed Graff's car was very thirsty on this trip. Here you see the men paving the street in Omer. Look at all those bags of cement.

We traveled on and soon crossed a little bridge. Henry remarked, "That's handy."

Graff, thinking he meant the bridge, said, "Yes, and I'll soon want to be sitting on one."

We all three laughed, but he didn't see the funny side of it, as we did. For what Henry saw was a "slop jar." Now laugh, old boy.

At 1:25 p.m., Graff sighed and said, "I'm too hungry to drive any farther. Let's park right here by these dandy little maples."

We pulled up and stopped by a nice spot that looked to have a shady area for our meal. I spread the robe on the ground and opened our "green safety can." Lucille and I prepared our lunch of bologna sandwiches, pickles, store-bought cookies, and bananas.

After we all ate, Lucille and I decided to cross the road, creep through a barbed wire fence, and look for water. Soon after, we returned bringing branches of huckleberries to the boys. They enjoyed their little surprise dessert.

Just then, a man and woman with a gray horse pulled up in their wagon and wanted to sell us huckleberries at $6 per bushel. We told them, "No room for them in the car." Tis a shame. I'd never seen so many wild berries.

We packed up and were on our way again. At 2:55 p.m., we reached Pinconning. Henry went into Allie Coggins store, found Mabel, and she came out with bottles of pop, which we all enjoyed. Henry bought a box of toothpicks for fear there wouldn't be any in Millington. Mabel told us, "You have eighteen miles to Bay City." We thanked her for her kindness and said, "Good-bye, Mabel."

At 3:30 p.m., Graff said, "Do you know we haven't had any punctures or tire troubles since we left home?" Don't brag, old boy, for we are a long way from home yet.

Soon we came across a big truck loaded with gravel tipped over in the ditch and had to wait for the men to loosen chains and let them down so we could pass. They certainly will have a time cleaning up that mess.

At 4:45 p.m., we drove through Indian Town. Graff waved his hand out the window as we passed a man standing on the corner. "Hello, Billy," he called to the big fellow. The man returned the friendly greeting in time as we continued on our way.

After reaching a good road, our driver picked up speed going at the rate of *forty-two miles per hour!* I looked back and noticed Henry seemed to be looking ahead for a soft spot to light on. I quietly laid my hand on Graff's arm and said, "Better be careful." And almost instantly, like a horse that is under control of his master, the Chevrolet fell back to its usual place and all breathed free again.

A big storm with dark gray clouds was approaching, and Graff thought if he drove slowly, it might pass ahead of us. Sure enough, it missed us, with only a few raindrops landing on us.

At 6:00 p.m. sharp, we arrived in Millington and into our yard at the Old Home. Henry got the key, jumped out, and unlocked the front door. He then came through the house and opened the back door for us to enter. Graff was tired out and suffering with a severe headache. He said, "I'm glad I didn't have to drive another mile."

Henry then built a fire in the kitchen stove, and I prepared our supper. We were all hungry and ate heartily at 7:00 p.m. Thalia, Vilas, and family came over to see us. After supper, I gave Graff's head a hard rubbing to relieve the pain, and he went to bed at 8:30 p.m.

Henry and I walked up to Mother and Father Van's house to find Henry's brother Fred and wife Madge Van Wagnen had arrived from Jackson that evening. We enjoyed a pleasant visit with all of them.

Wednesday, June 29, 1921

All up and had a big breakfast after a good night's rest. The cots were fine for camping, but I was glad to sleep on my feather bed once again. Henry went out into the backyard and looked over the garden while the rest of us visited indoors for a while. We also had various items to sort through and put away from our trip. Graff talked of going home, but Henry came in and said, "There are lots of nice ripe red raspberries out in the patch."

I said, "Go out and pick some, and we'll have a nice shortcake before Graff goes home."

So I hustled to make the biscuits and put the kettle on, while Lucille set the table with plates, spoons, cups and saucers, and a small pitcher of fresh cream. The boys came in with a good amount of berries, which I quickly rinsed and put into a large bowl with an ample amount of sugar. Soon we all sat down to have a good square meal of fresh raspberry shortcake and hot tea. I can't remember anything tasting a good as that did.

After everyone had eaten their fill, we went back out to the patch to pick some raspberries for Graff to take home. The bushes were loaded with ripe berries and it didn't take long for us to have two full quarts.

At 2:30 p.m., Graff decided it was time to go and gathered up his luggage. Henry and I followed him as he stepped out our kitchen door, onto the porch and out to the car. He turned to us and said, "Now, I must be going. I hate to get into the car alone after the good time we've all had together, for it is a long ride alone and a lonesome place when I get home." We saw the sad expression begin to return to Graff's face.

Henry placed his hand on Graff's shoulder and said, "Don't stay away too long, but when you get lonesome, run out to the car and come and see us. You are always welcome."

Then with a gentle handclasp and a "good-bye, Graff," he stepped into the car. He took his seat behind the wheel and the Chevy moved out onto the street, around the corner to the north and passed from our sight.

In this the closing chapter of my little book, I want to say that I have endeavored to write down many little incidents and funny sayings that have happened along our way. Many things, that perhaps were entirely missed by the others of our party, or in a short time forgotten, that will always remain with me in memory. For like the old saying:

You may break, you may shatter the vase,
if you will,
But the scent of the roses will hang round it still.

So will the memory of all those pleasant, happy, restful hours remain with me in the coming years. And I shall always remember them as some of the happiest along my journey through life.

Chapter 7
Fireflies

Looking Back to the 1880s

Juniata Township Farms—July 1887

Ethel Bailey (13 years old), Graff Gawne (17 years old), and four other Gawne children were walking on the narrow, dirt road back home to their farms. Alma, (14), George (12), Cyrus (10), and Laura (8) had been enjoying the late afternoon together after their chores. It was a warm, clear night and getting dark now, but since their older brother Graff was with them, their parents had no need to worry.

They came to the meadow between the family farms when suddenly Laura exclaimed, "Look, the fireflies are out!" The other children spotted them at once. The large meadow was alive with hundreds of tiny lights drifting up from the tall grass. The little creatures were flying slowly up and then their "light" would fade out.

"Let's catch them," George and Cyrus said almost at the same time. And with that, they all took off running into the meadow, grasping at the lights and laughing as most of them were missing.

Then Graff announced, "I've got one." He held up his right clenched fist for all to see as he slowly opened his hand and the little light buzzed away.

"No, Graff," protested Laura. "We want to keep them."

The other children agreed, and Ethel even found herself chiming in. "We need something to put them in."

Graff chuckled at the childish idea, but then turned to the boys and said, "Go home and get some jars or bottles."

George and Cyrus both agreed and immediately ran back toward the Gawne farm excitedly chattering as they went. When they had reached the tree line and were disappearing from view, one of them turned back and yelled, “Save some for us!”

Ethel laughed at the thought that they might run out of them as she tried to grab one. To her surprise, she caught it in her hand and held it.

I'll put it in my pocket, she thought as she pushed her hand down the small opening in her skirt. She carefully opened her hand and pulled it out as she put her other hand on top to hold it in.

The others meantime were running and jumping as they grabbed at the bugs that didn't seem a bit aware that they were being pursued. After a few tries, they were all getting good at judging how the bugs would fly up slowly and then they would swipe at them before their little light went out.

“I got one!” was heard, then another “Me too!” among the laughter and calls of “There are some over here.” Graff was enjoying watching this scene and occasionally would reach out and easily grab a bug. He was also instructing Laura on the proper technique.

Just then, Ethel looked toward her home and saw her older sister, Ella, standing near the barn, bathed in moonlight and easily spotted. She had been amused as she stood watching the children.

Ethel called to her, “Ella, bring a couple of jars.”

Even though her sister was seven years older, she wasn't going to miss this chance to have some fun. Ella immediately turned and ran for the house, knowing Mama would gladly give her something to use.

The two boys returned running and gasping as they showed everyone the two jars they found. Ella soon arrived at the field with two large canning jars, and the children brought their treasures over and began depositing the glowing creatures inside. Ethel thought the little lights looked even prettier through the pale green glass.

Squeals were heard from time to time as the bugs landed and crawled on a hand or face, but mostly the announcements were: “I've got another one! Bring the jar. Keep your hand on top. Don't let them out!”

Ethel and Ella worked as a team and were collecting as many as the children and having just as much fun, if the truth be told. The children were running to them, putting in more bugs as fast as they caught them.

After some time had gone by, Graff said loudly, "I think we've got enough. Time to head home."

Ethel looked his way and secretly cherished the way Graff looked in the moonlight. He was so dear to her, and seeing how he loved his brothers and sisters warmed her heart.

"Just a few more, please, Graff?" begged the children. "I need more in my jar."

When Graff finally gathered everyone together, they all compared their catches. Ethel and Ella had fourteen in one jar and fifteen in the other. They had counted as they filled the jars. The best they could figure, the other two jars had twenty in one and fifteen in the smaller one. The children were admiring their jars and watching the little lights when Ethel said, "Here, take one of our jars. You all helped fill it."

"Hooray" and "Thank you, Ethel," was heard as she handed it to them.

Alma asked Ethel, "What are you going to do with your jar?"

Without hesitation, she said, "I'm going to put a top on it and set it on my bedroom dresser by the window. Won't that be pretty in the dark tonight?"

"Yes!" all the children agreed, saying they were going to do the same. Laura was nearly wild with excitement as she thought of it, and she jumped up and down until Graff had to start walking toward home.

"Let's go," he said. "We'll put one jar in the girls' room, one jar in the boys' room and give one jar to Mother." The group happily agreed as they waved and said their good-byes.

Ethel and Ella turned and linked arms as they walked through the field and headed toward home. They laughed as they agreed that they hadn't had so much fun in quite some time. As they walked from the field into the yard, Ethel was careful to keep her hand firmly on top of her jar.

Back at the house, they were excited to show off their catch to Mama, who was quietly sitting in her rocker doing some mending. She looked up from the dim lantern light as the girls giggled and started telling her about their adventure.

"Shhhh... girls, your papa is asleep," she whispered as she stood up and looked closely at the jar. The bugs were busily flying and crawling around in it and sending out their little lights. She smiled and kissed her girls good-night. "Be sure to cover that jar real good. I don't want those things loose in the house."

"We will, Mama," Ethel said as she and her sister headed for their bedroom. After stepping inside, they shut the door, and Ethel handed the jar to Ella to hold while she walked to the dresser and opened the top drawer. After a moment of digging around, she pulled out a small, white hanky.

"This should work," she said as she walked back in the darkened room and placed the hanky over the top and down over the edge. "We need something to tie it off. Look for a ribbon or string," she whispered.

Ella headed for a small box on top of the table next to the bed quickly returning with a thin blue ribbon just the right length to tie around the hanky. The sisters smiled at each other as Ella finished off their special lamp with a neat little bow, and Ethel took the jar and set it on top of the dresser next to the window. The room was quite dark except for the light of the full moon streaming through the window.

The girls changed into their nightgowns and climbed into the large bed they shared. It was so warm in the room that they agreed to lay on top of the covers. Resting back on their pillows, they looked at the sparkling jar by the window. It was far enough away that they couldn't tell there were bugs inside; just beautiful little flashing lights. It was so peaceful laying there with only the sounds of crickets chirping in the night.

Ethel smiled as she remembered all the fun she had just shared with her sister and neighbor friends. She thought about the excitement on the children's faces; their hot, sweaty hands; and the meadow in the moonlight so bright it cast shadows. Her heart was warmed when she remembered how Graff looked, tending to his flock of brothers and sisters. She had, however, quite forgotten about the firefly that was still crawling around in her skirt pocket.

The two sisters talked and laughed quietly for a while, discussing the moments of their day. These talks weren't as frequent as they had been in the past. Ella was a young woman now and soon to be married. Ethel didn't like the thought of her sister leaving and couldn't imagine what it would be like without her. That was sort of a selfish thought, but she couldn't help it because she loved her sister and would miss her terribly.

She lay in bed for some time thinking and soon heard her sister breathing slowly and realized she had fallen asleep. Gazing sleepy-eyed at the jar across the room, she cherished the memory of this day. The fireflies' blinking lights seemed to be fuzzy as she finally closed her eyes and drifted off to sleep.

Chapter 8
Golden Memories

Now, if you have read the contents of the little "books" I have written for you, I will endeavor to continue the story of many other happy days that we have spent together since then.

Wednesday, July 6, 1921

At 7:00 p.m., we heard the sound of the Chevrolet pulling in the driveway. Grafton stepped out and said, "Where is Willard? I thought it was time for him to go on a short vacation, and I've come down to take him home with me."

Willard happily accepted the invitation, and after spending the night, the boys left Thursday morning. They stepped out of the front door, down the steps and out to the roadside where the good old Chevy stood in readiness for the homeward run to Midland.

Both did their share in making each one enjoy the other fellow's company until Saturday, July 16, when they again started back to Millington. Both thought they could detect the odor of fried cakes in the air.

It seems that Graff had done something to the muffler on the Chevrolet. I judge from the way they told me the ladies stepped along as they passed by that the muffler had not been put out of commission. Willard said one lady seemed so glad to see them that she held her umbrella high in the air. Well, laugh if you want to, he said I could talk to the lady and she would vouch for the fact.

Sunday, July 17, 1921

All up and had breakfast. We got ready and attended the Methodist-Episcopal Church service at 10:30 a.m. I invited Mrs. Patterson to walk home with me. And later while I prepared my lunch to take with us, I asked her to go with us for the afternoon drive, which she gladly consented to.

Shortly after 1:00 p.m., we locked the doors and with lunch basket in hand, we walked out into the back yard where the Chevy was in waiting. I took my seat beside the driver, and Mrs. Patterson and Henry occupied the backseat. Lucille and Loyal followed us with his car.

We drove out east on the familiar dirt road that led us back to the "Old Homestead" on the banks of Houghton Creek, where the happiest days of my life were spent. As we drew nearer, I saw the old familiar places and thought of the dear ones that had meant so much to me in those happy years. Tears filled my eyes and crept silently down my cheeks.

We crossed the bridge, and on up the hill where on the right side of the road we parked the cars. Graff was the first one out, leaving us and going back the same direction from which we had just come. Creeping through the wire fence and bending down, he cleaned out the leaves from the old spring. Then quietly passed along and into the bushes where he disappeared from our sight.

We followed down the same hillside path and I crept through the fence and went to the old spring. I found the same cool sparkling water running slowly from the bank where it ran so many, many years ago. This was the place where so often in my girlhood days, I had carried pail after pail of the same refreshing water to the dear ones who were with me then, but who have now gone out and away from me.

Henry said, "Ethel, why didn't you bring a cup so you could get a drink from this spring you have talked about so many times? Why, it looks as though it has been cleaned out purposely for your benefit."

We did not know until weeks later that it was Graff's hands that had carefully picked out all the leaves and little sticks, leaving the water flowing fresh and clean.

Then we passed on down the hill and onto the bridge. Here in our young days, Graff and I had often stood and looked into the waters below. Lucille, with her Kodak in hand told us, "You two get ready and I'll take your picture."

Graff helped me up on the iron railing, and she took this picture.

After this, we crossed the bridge down over the old driveway at the side, along the water's edge where we groped our way along among the boughs and branches of the trees. We finally stood on the point of ground near where the little stream rippled and sang as it floated along and later joined the waters of the Cass River.

Here along this little stream, I had spent many happy hours beneath the tall maple trees that used to stand here side by side and where Graff and I had stood and carved our names long years ago.

Today, we found to our sorrow, the maples under which we had spent so many happy hours, were gone. But not far from where they used to stand, two others had grown also side by side. We sat down there, and Lucille took this picture.

No doubt we were both thinking of the changes that had come into our lives and how much sadness and heartache we had both passed through since the time we had last sat near this same spot, beneath the maples.

Here along the banks of this little babbling brook, I had often wandered. Here at the twilight hour, when his work for the day was done, Graff often found me. Our home was his home during those years, and he came to me; the one who was his friend, counselor, and companion. I was the one who shared all his joys and sorrows and the bright hope of what the future would bring to him.

Little did he realize all the long, long years of sadness that were in store for him, or that when we met again on this same spot many years later, my heavy mass of golden hair would be thickly threaded with silver gray.

We finally headed back to the Old Homestead on the hill. Here at the west end of the house, in the same old pathway where we had walked so many times, Lucille took another picture.

Behind us stands the old barn my father built in August of 1887. In front of us is the same old path that led down to the gate. But alas, the dear old gate we both remember so well is gone and another stands in its place. Just here so many memories come back to me that I think of these old words:

Backward turn backward, oh Time in your flight.
Make me a girl again, just for tonight.

Chapter 9
Ethel and Graff

Looking Back to the 1880s

The Bailey Farm—Vassar, Michigan
September 1887

Grafton Gawne was determined as he walked through the field from his home to the Bailey farm next to it. He had put in a long day in hot weather and was feeling relieved it was done. The young man was used to hard work, but today seemed to be especially dragged out. Now he could look forward to a pleasant evening with his dear friend, Ethel. She was three years his junior, having just turned fourteen, but not at all like the other silly girls her age. Ethel was special to him in so many ways, and he couldn't wait any longer to tell her so. He quickened his pace and looked ahead at the Bailey house and saw her standing on the porch. He was still some distance from her, but he could see her sweet smile.

Even though the sun would be setting soon, Graff squinted against the harsh sunlight as he made his way. Ethel had been in his thoughts all day as he worked the farm and now he was about to greet her in their friendly way.

Ethel brushed back a lock of her hair from her forehead and quickly tucked in the loose ends that had fallen from her bun. She kept her eyes on Graff as she smoothed and straightened her skirt. She and Graff had been friends and neighbors for some time, but now she felt he was becoming much more than a friend. He was so quiet and shy at times; it was hard for her to tell if it was just her imagination or if he had special feelings for her. She was, in her mind, quite ready to be courted. Just the thought of that made her blush a little.

As he got closer to the Bailey farmhouse, Graff thought of what he would say to Ethel. He had never had any trouble talking to her before, but this was different. What if she laughed at him thinking he was joking with her as he often did? Maybe she would be surprised and not at all pleased, or think he was being forward.

Ethel stepped out from the porch and waved at Graff who was now through the field and entering the barnyard.

"Hello, Laddie," she called to him, using the name her papa had given him. Both her parents thought the world of Graff and considered him a part of their family. He was much more than *the neighbor boy* to them.

"Hello," Graff called back.

Ethel stayed where she was and enjoyed watching Graff as he walked toward her. She smiled and noticed how tanned his face was from all the hours working in the sun. Just as Graff approached, Mrs. Bailey opened the screen door from the kitchen and stepped on to the porch. Weary from the day's work and the heat from the kitchen, she breathed a sigh and said, "Well, Graff, how do you do this fine evening?"

"Just fine, Mrs. Bailey. It sure was a hot one today," Graff replied as he glanced her way then back to Ethel.

"Yes, indeed. How are your folks? Your mama still feeling poorly?"

"They're doing just fine. Said to tell you thanks for the biscuits you sent over."

"Don't mention it, Graff. We had plenty that day, and we sure couldn't eat them all. Can't figure why I ended up making so many..." Her voice trailed off as she leaned on the railing and looked off in the distance.

By now, Ethel was intent on ending the biscuit conversation and slipping off with Graff as they often did. She looked at him and it seemed he had the same idea when he tilted his head toward the direction of the grove of maple trees between their homes. She stepped forward as Graff turned and walked beside her, heading across the yard without another word to her mother.

The two strolled along in silence for a while, each of them with thoughts of the many times they had taken this walk before. But this time seemed different. Both of them had things they could say, but somehow there was something stopping them.

They soon reached the coolness of the maples, and next to them the little stream could be heard babbling contently over the rocks. There were many trees growing so closely together that hardly any sunlight reached the ground below their full branches. It was so peaceful there, with only the chirps of the different birds singing their melodies to each other. *Love birds*, thought Ethel. Finally, Graff decided to break the silence.

"Come look at this, Ethel," he said as he walked over to one of the larger trees. She followed him and stood next to him facing the tree. Before she could question him about it, he pulled something from the pocket of his overalls. He was still looking at the tree when he opened his pocketknife and began to carve into the bark.

Ethel watched as the first few letters were appearing. G-R-A... She guessed it would be GRAFF, and soon he had finished his name.

"That's good, Graff," she said without knowing he wasn't finished.

As he continued with the next letter underneath his name. Ethel assumed it was going to be his last name: GAWNE. Suddenly, she realized he was making the letter E... then T-H... She watched as he finished her name and then carved a small heart beside it. Graff brushed off the bark that was clinging to the letters and closed his knife. He slipped it back into his pocket and turned to look at Ethel. She was so pretty standing there with her honey-blond hair and pale blue eyes he loved so much.

"Oh, Graff," she whispered as she reached her hand to touch his arm. Without another word, Graff leaned down and did what he had been thinking about all day. He kissed her. Ethel was taken by surprise, but not before she closed her eyes and was thrilled by her very first kiss.

The two stayed under the maples for some time, talking as the evening shadows lengthened over the meadow. As the sun finally set, Graff pulled Ethel to him and held her in his arms.

"We should be getting back," he said softly. Saying this was against everything he was feeling, but he cared too much for Ethel to linger there any longer.

They walked hand in hand back to the farmhouse, both of them hating to part. When they reached the porch, they reluctantly said their good-nights, and Graff turned and made his way home.

That night, after the rest of the family was sleeping, Ethel lay quietly in bed and relived all the sweet moments of this day, especially the kiss. She was so happy she thought she would float away. Tomorrow would seem so different now that she was in love and living so near to her sweetheart.

Should she tell her sister Ella about this? Would it be proper to inform her parents? She had no way of knowing that her folks had already guessed there was a special attachment between her and Graff. This news really wouldn't come as any surprise to them. As all these thoughts swirled around in her mind, Ethel knew one thing for sure. *She would remember this day for the rest of her life.*

Chapter 10
Midland Visit

Sunday, July 17, 1921
Our trip to the Old Homestead at Vassar, Michigan

We all continued on with our visit to my home where I grew up as a girl, and we went out east of the house where Lucille took several more pictures.

Here is the one of Henry and I beneath the cluster of maple trees where Henry had sat with my father in 1892 and asked for his consent to marry me.

After taking pictures, we all went through the barbed wire fence and got into the cars and drove east to find George Pearson, an old English friend. I just love to listen to him when he speaks in that distinctive manner. "Jolly good, don't you think?"

He came out and after hearty greetings all around, Graff and Loyal parked the cars. Then with the boys and Henry to help, we moved the big workbench which we used for a table, and soon we had our dinner ready. Everyone was hungry by now and dinner tasted good to all.

As we started for home, Graff remembered that the muffler was still in working order just as we passed a couple of ladies. Graff revved the engine, making a sudden loud rumble. One lady almost tore her skirt off she jerked it so quickly as she jumped to one side to let us pass! We all laughed until our sides were sore.

Monday, July 18, 1921

All up and enjoyed a nice big breakfast of bacon and eggs, toast, strawberry jam, and hot tea. At 8:00 a.m., Lucille went up town to the newspaper office while Graff headed out to the Chevy and back to Midland. *Good-bye dear friend, come back soon.*

Friday, July 29, 1921

At 4:45 p.m., I had been visiting with my oldest sister Lois (whom we always call "Ret"). *Don't ask me how she came by that name. It's been so long ago.* She was here to spend a few days, and I had been looking forward to her visit.

At the same time, we were watching what appeared to be a bad storm approaching. Soon the wind began to blow, and I hurried upstairs to close the windows. On my way, I heard and recognized the sound of the Chevy as it rounded the corner from the north and Graff hurriedly drove into the yard. Just then, the storm broke with wind, thunder, lightning, and pouring rain! Needless to say, we all headed for cover.

Ret had not seen Graff in several years, but for all that, no introductions were needed. It is not necessary to say anything about our visit, for we all kept busy. Ret and I talked hour after hour way into the night.

Poor Henry couldn't half sleep. He doesn't seem to understand what we could possibly be talking about so long at our little "hen parties." Ha ha.

Saturday, July 30, 1921

Twas a busy day as usual for me. I baked four loaves of bread, two peach pies and put a pork roast, carrots, and potatoes in the oven to have for dinner. Graff invited us to go for a drive in the afternoon, but Ret thought it was too warm, so we continued visiting at home. Henry and Graff got the checkerboard out and played several quiet games in the parlor.

Sunday, July 31, 1921

We did not attend church this morning but stayed home and prepared dinner. Sunday afternoon, Graff went over to Thalia's and kept watch of the babies for her to attend the funeral of Ray Henderson, whose body returned from overseas Thursday eve, July 28. Henry and I also attended and were very saddened for the Henderson family and their loss.

After the funeral, we came home with Thalia and visited awhile. Theo and little Billy were well-behaved according to Graff, although I think he was kept very busy giving "horsey rides."

We returned home later to have our supper and after dessert and tea, Graff left for Midland at 8:00 p.m.

Friday, August 12, 1921

Ret and I spent the afternoon uptown enjoying the sights of the Millington Homecoming, and finally, we decided we were ready to come home. We found Lucille and Loyal just getting ready for a drive, and they asked Ret to go with them. She happily agreed, but upon backing out into the roadway, the brakes did not work and his car rolled into the touring car of Albert Wilcox. Thankfully, no serious damage was done—just one bent fender.

Sunday, August 14, 1921

All up at an early hour for us on Sunday due to our plans to drive to Hunters Creek today. We had breakfast and hustled our housework. I slipped a sack of fried cakes, one jellyroll cake, and two-dozen nice sandwiches in my basket. Soon we were all ready and out to the car.

We drove south to Lapeer, where we stopped at Henry's brother Olin and wife Fory Van Wagnen's home. We spotted Olin as he started across the ball ground in back of his home on his way uptown. We finally attracted his attention, and he came back to the house. We all got out and inspected the new basement, etc. Fory was just getting up and dressed hurriedly and came out with us. After a short visit with them, brother Olin directed us which road to take to Hunters Creek and on we went.

We reached the Hance home shortly after 11:00 a.m. Having expected our visit, they were watching for us and received us with open arms. Jerome and Hattie popped out of the door and off the front porch like a shot out of a gun! Henry was the first one out of the car, and he had only just hit the ground when his cousin Hattie captured him at the first bound and held him captive with both arms around his neck, while the kisses fell thick and fast upon his lips and face.

Jerome looked on quietly for a few seconds and then sprang quickly to the side of the car and said, "I guess there are others that can play the game, dear cousin Ethel." And took me in his arms and kissed me. Lucille was next and also received a good big hugging.

Graff sat still in the front seat during these few minutes and when the first wild rush was over, I turned to him and said, "Come, Grafton." He at once stepped out and I said, "This is Hattie and Jerome, whom you have so often heard me speak of. And this is Mr. Gawne, or just plain Graff, *our dearest friend.*"

We then all entered the front door and there we met their grown children Leon and Beatrice, and soon all were visiting. "The Big Four", as I named the boys, went into the parlor, and we felt at once that none were strangers to the other.

We girls soon got busy with preparations for dinner, for somehow I had a sort of hungry feeling in my stomach. And when we had dinner on the table, the boys were just as anxious to eat as we were and although this picture was not taken just at that time, this is just what Graff looked like after he had eaten his dinner and said when Hattie passed him a second piece of pie.

"Thanks, but it's no use. I couldn't eat another bite." And I believed him, while I also felt sorry for Lucille, for I'm sure she was in misery.

Of course, Hattie and I had taken our time and so did not gorge ourselves so quickly, and I guess were able to eat just as much or maybe more than the others by taking our time. Beatrice got the start of us while she and Lucille were in the kitchen and got away with a few of my fried cakes. I couldn't say *how many*, for neither Hattie nor I had counted them.

In the afternoon, the boys went out and looked the farm over, and later, we all went to the barn and were weighed. But, maybe it would be best not to say anything more about that. Ha ha.

About 3:30 p.m., we left for home feeling that it had proved to be one of the happiest days we had spent during the summer. When we were all out beside the car, Hattie said, "Grafton, I want to kiss you good-bye, for you must never feel you are a stranger to us anymore." And true to the mood, she raised her face to his and kissed his lips, then said, "God bless you. You'll come again, won't you?"

His eyes filled with tears and he said, "I surely will if I live, for I feel as though I'll want to come as badly as the others did, and I don't blame them."

We returned home by way of North Branch. On our way, we stopped at the home of James McKenzie. We drove in the yard and when we entered the house and Mrs. McKenzie discovered it was Graff with us, she said, "Why, Graff Gawne, is this you?"

He replied, "It surely is."

"Well, I'm going to kiss you." And for the second time that day, he was kissed by another man's wife. *So, I'm not the only one that greets him with a friendly kiss.*

A little later, Mrs. McKenzie slipped away to the kitchen, fixed the fire, and prepared a lunch that we all greatly enjoyed.

We continued our visit going back to the years of Graff's young manhood when he was both father and mother to his brothers and sisters after the death of his own dear mother. Mr. and Mrs. McKenzie, like myself, knew how hard those years had been and what it had meant to him in fulfilling his dying mother's request when she had said to him, "*Grafton, look after the children.*"

And we were not ashamed of the tears that coursed down our cheeks as we recalled those sad days of long ago.

Finally, we said farewell to the McKenzies and returned home at 8:00 p.m. feeling somewhat tired. Soon we all retired to bed with the agreement that we had enjoyed every minute of the day.

Monday, August 15, 1921

All up at the usual hour, but I do not wash on certain Mondays. Henry often laughs and says, "Well, there won't be any washing done today."

Graff left for Midland at 4:00 p.m. Just before starting, he said, "I'll run in someday and bring you some nice cucumbers for pickles, so don't buy any." Henry has often said those were the best dill pickles we ever had. *Thank you.*

Thursday, August 25, 1921

Graff started for Caro to attend the county fair, putting in about three bushels of cucumbers to bring to Millington. He expected to enjoy the fair during the day and then drive down home and stay overnight. But, he had all kinds of bad luck. First, he had two blow outs and did not reach Caro till late, at about 9:00 p.m. Then he decided it was time to start south, and shortly afterwards, his lights burned out and he thought by running carefully and a little slower, he could go on. But, alas, some other fellow had been unfortunate too and had left his car beside the road, and Graff did not see it in time to avoid a crash, which brought his old Chevy to a *standstill.* Fortunately, he was not injured, but it cost him $30 for repairs on the Chevy.

He was lucky by having a friend drive up who took him several miles on his way. He went to his brother Al's, and he returned with him for his car. The next morning, Graff took Al's sedan and came on to Millington, stopping to deliver the cucumbers and only stayed about a half an hour, then hurried back to Vassar.

Saturday, September 3, 1921

About 1:00 p.m., we were surprised to see the front door open and the big laddie step in. He said, "No, I haven't had my dinner, and I'm as hungry as a bear. I can only wait long enough to eat, for I want to catch the autobus to Vassar. I've been to Otisville on a collection trip for White of Saginaw."

So I quickly put dinner on for him. It was a short but pleasant visit, and Graff knows he is welcome to stop in *anytime.*

Tuesday, September 6, 1921

This was Henry's first day on the job at the gristmill in Millington. After work that evening, while Henry was sitting near the Ford garage about 7:30 p.m. visiting with some men, he caught a glimpse of someone going into the garage. When he came out, he discovered it was Graff. So they jumped back in the car and they both came home. Henry stayed only a few minutes because he had to go to IOOF Lodge meeting.

I prepared lunch for Graff and afterwards, we spent the evening visiting until Henry came home from the lodge. We all enjoyed a piece of pie and a glass of milk before retiring. Graff left for home in the Chevy at 10:00 a.m. the next morning.

Sunday, September 18, 1921

Graff drove in just before supper last night so we would have everything in readiness for our trip to Hunters Creek this morning. We got up a little later than we planned, but when we did get busy, everything was put into place in a hurry and soon all was packed for the long drive.

When we were almost ready to go, Lucille decided she would rather stay home and sleep, so I sent Henry over to see if Thalia would go with us. She gladly accepted our invitation and hurried over. At last we were ready to leave about 8:15 a.m.

We soon arrived in North Branch where we called at Henry's sister Flossie and husband Jesse Raphley's home and received an invitation to stop on our return and have supper with them. We left there going south over fourteen miles of gravel road into Attica where Henry's cousin Hattie and husband Jerome Hance resided. At the Hance farm home, we received the heartiest welcome and enjoyed a chicken dinner with gravy and biscuits. And oh my, how they all did eat, hardly taking time to pass me what I asked for. We left for North Branch about 3:30 p.m. and had a nice visit with Henry's sister Flossie and husband Jesse and enjoyed her lovely supper. Shortly after eating our second bountiful meal of the day, we left for home, reaching there about 7:30 p.m. Thus ended one more pleasant Sunday for all of us.

Wednesday, September 21, 1921

We rose up a little earlier than usual this morning. Graff had come late last night, and we are ready to step into the Chevy at 8:30 a.m.

Graff took his place at the wheel, and Henry and I were on our way with him to Midland. We enjoyed our ride going by way of Saginaw where we stopped to shop at the Wm. Barie store. There I bought a new winter coat that I was in need of for the price of $27. It is a beautiful dark green wool with a gathered waist band. The high collar and long hem should keep me warm this winter. It seemed that some of the newer styles were too short for me. I noticed dress lengths were also creeping up to the knees. *Mercy!*

After shopping, we then entered the car and left for Midland. We passed along the banks of the Tittabawassee River. There, its waters floated merrily along and the trees cast cool shadows where the cattle stood and enjoyed themselves in the water.

Midland Home

We moved along swiftly reaching Graff's home at Midland just at the noon hour where we found Hod and Amy Davis just eating dinner. Graff and Hod went to the store and meat market and after their return we soon had our dinner. While we were yet at the table, a man came to the door and wanted to speak to Graff. He went out and in fifteen minutes made a deal for a ten-acre piece of ground not far from his home. He took Henry for a witness, and with the man and his wife, they drove down and made out the papers. I stayed at home and enjoyed Amy's companionship and thus the time passed until the boys returned. After supper, we all visited and talked about Graff's plans for his new property.

Then, about 9:30 p.m., I begged to be excused as I felt rather tired after the long, cool ride. I mounted the stairs, and in a few minutes, I was enjoying myself in a nice warm feather bed. Henry and Graff stayed downstairs and visited until 11:30 p.m. when Henry finally came up to bed. Graff wrote Lucille a letter to let her know that we arrived home okay. Then we heard him come carefully up the stairs and along the hallway as he passed into his room. Thus ended the first day of our stay in Midland. *Sleep well everyone.*

Thursday, September 22, 1921

All up and stirring at a reasonable hour and ready for breakfast when Amy called us to the table. The morning seemed much warmer than yesterday, so Graff said to get ready and we would get down to the Fairgrounds early. So, at 10:00 a.m., the Chevy once more moved out onto the highway and downtown to the Midland Fairgrounds. Graff got tickets, and we drove in and parked opposite the grandstand. The grounds were already bustling with people wandering back and forth through the barns. We decided to head over to see the livestock when we came upon this little girl who proudly posed with her pig.

It wasn't long after, I looked and near the end of a barn I saw Charlie Rutherford, an old schoolmate of mine from Vassar. I hadn't seen him in years. When we approached him, his face lit up and he called, "Why, *Ethel Bailey!* What brings you here?" I laughed and introduced him to Henry and Graff. After a short visit, we went into a large barn area where we saw a hog that was raised at a county farm weighing 1,200 pounds! There were also some dandy little piglets in a pen, which we enjoyed looking at. Henry noted that it wouldn't be long and they would make some fine bacon. We finished viewing, then went out near the grandstand and had dinner at Mrs. Pettit's stand. After we satisfied our hunger, we returned to the track and watched the races. Benny Tripp, a hunchback, won the race with his horse. "Cheers, cheers for Benny and his horse!"

After enjoying a good many races and such, we had our supper at the IOOF counter and the meal was fine. Then we all returned to the car where we stood and watched the balloon ascension. It was a thrilling site to behold. Later, we returned to Graff's home after an enjoyable evening. We were all tired and agreed to *hit the hay* early for a good night's rest.

Friday, September, 23, 1921

About 10:00 a.m., we drove to downtown Midland where Graff went into the bank and got the money left there to pay for the cucumbers. He came back and gave it to me to count. Just as I finished my task, a big fine-looking gentleman came up and said, "Hello, Grafton. Where have you been? I've been looking all over for you."

Graff said, "Dr. Lambie, meet my friends from Millington, Henry and Ethel Van Wagnen." We enjoyed a few minutes visiting, and before leaving us, the doctor urged Graff to come to the lodge meeting that night.

We then drove through town and over to the Crow's Nest and parked the car by the barn. The boys gathered a nice mess of evergreen corn, which we will enjoy for our Saturday dinner. After an inspection of the interior of the barn, we returned to the car and drove to the fairgrounds.

Graff bought tickets for the grandstand, and we stopped at a counter to have our dinner before settling into our seats. There were so many after Graff that we insisted that he go and enjoy the sports with his friends. Henry and I went up to the grandstand to view the Masons and IOOF men gather for a *tug-of-war.*

We watched Graff being one of the Odd Fellows against the Masons. Oh how we laughed until I felt I would not be able to ride back to the farm unless the end came soon. The pull lasted about ten minutes before the Odd Fellows got started and when they did, the Masons had to go their way. Some of them tumbled to the ground in defeat. After the feat of strength was over, Graff made his way up to us in the grandstand; pretty well winded but glad his side had won.

A little later, there came the announcement of the *Great Tomato Battle.* We all watched the men that came out and placed two bushels of ripe tomatoes at the right and two bushels at the left. Then nine Odd Fellows took their place on one side and nine Masons on the other. At the signal, one-two-three *Go!* They began pelting each other with those ripe tomatoes! It was a gory battle, which lasted several minutes, and finally the Masons drove the Odd Fellows over the line, and the cheers were given to the winners. It was well it ended when it did, or Henry and Graff would surely have needed the attention of a doctor they laughed so.

Later that evening, after leaving the fairgrounds, we all decided we would go to the theatre. We enjoyed a movie called *The Kid* with Charlie Chaplin, who was wonderful in his part.

It was late when we returned to Graff's home, so I hunted around the kitchen and found Amy's cookies. We enjoyed some and then went upstairs quietly so as not to disturb Hod and Amy who were sleeping.

Saturday, September 24, 1921

About 10:30 a.m., we drove to downtown Midland. The boys left me at one store to make some purchases for the grandchildren Theo and Billy, while they went on somewhere else. While in the store, I spotted a nice auto basket that just suited me, so while I was waiting, the boys finally returned and found me standing outside. I told Henry that he could go in and buy me the basket as a keepsake.

I said, "It will cost you $1.25."

So he went in and soon returned with the basket telling Graff, "Ethel will likely be slipping that in the car with lunch in it for some of our trips." He guessed correctly.

Then we went home and had dinner, but oh my—*Green corn!* Sweetness. I had put it on to boil for two long hours and when we took it out of the kettle for dinner, it looked as blue as a person does when they are having a hard chill.

After dinner, I got busy in *the Office* and soon had things all stirred up. When the boys came in from the barn, I called Graff and invited him to sort papers, etc. He did his part and then left for some other chores. Then I swept, dusted, rearranged books and papers, and fixed up the desk with a general cleanup. After that, I washed the windows, and as a finishing touch, I went outside and gathered flowers for a bouquet. I found a pretty vase in the cellar, filled it with water, and arranged the flowers in it. It was such a nice variety of red roses and orange and pink zinnias. They certainly looked lovely as I placed them on his desk, walked out, and closed the door.

Later in the afternoon, the men returned to the house, and Graff opened the door to his office. The surprised yet pleased look that came into his eyes and face paid for all the pains I had taken to put his room in order. *Many thanks, Ethel.*

Then, once more, we entered the car and drove downtown across the big bridge that spans the river. Read that sign on top of the bridge, old boy. You might want to slow down!

$10 Fine For Riding or Driving On This Bridge Faster Than A Walk

On we went for several miles out near Posyville, and finally returned to Graff's home to have supper. Afterwards, we drove downtown and enjoyed a good show and then back home to have a late lunch. I drank up nearly all of Graff's big cup of milk. "First come, first served," the saying goes. And even though I was second, Graff gave it to me, and I enjoyed it too. It just saved me from going to bed hungry. *I thank you. Good-night, Laddie boy.*

During the night, it rained, the wind blew, and then turned cold. Graff's dog "Tige" must have gotten lonesome outside and began to howl. Graff raised his bedroom window, and if the dog had not awakened me, Graff surely would have done so when he stuck his head out and hollered,

"You lay down and keep still!" And he did.

Chapter 11
The Lord Giveth

Looking Back to the 1880s

The Gawne Family Farm—April 1888

Mrs. Olive Gawne was expecting her ninth child any day now. She was feeling very worn out lately and hoped the baby would come soon. Today, she decided to have her children help her arrange some things in her bedroom, thinking it might help them accept the new arrival into their home. She had the girls—Alma, Laura, Olive, and little Myrtle—arrange the diapers, nightgowns, sleeping bonnets, and whatnot on a table set up near the bed. The older girls realized that there would be some changes in the household, but five-year-old Olive and three-year-old Myrtle seemed to think their Mama was going to bring them some sort of baby doll for them to play with. Alma had a time keeping them from fussing with the nightgowns and such. She carefully refolded the diapers in a nice neat pile and instructed them not to touch. Being the oldest girl, she took it upon herself to get everything in order.

Graff and the younger boys, George, Cyrus, and Alfred Jr., carried the large wooden cradle in and set it down next to the big bed where Mama showed them. She had some quilts and small blankets that she laid in the cradle, and before she knew it, Olive and Myrtle were trying to climb in to play.

Mrs. Gawne noticed that her children seemed to be taking this soon-to-be event in different ways. The younger boys didn't appear too excited about the new arrival into their family, except thirteen-year-old George who proclaimed he hoped it wasn't *another girl.* That's all it took for the siblings to start the tit-for-tat on who was better: boys or girls. Graff took notice of his mother's weariness with all the racket and said loudly, "That's enough *helping* for now. What say we all go outside and find something to do?"

At that, the children all agreed and happily bounded out of the room, leaving Mrs. Gawne somewhat relieved as she smiled a silent *thank you* to Graff. Despite the latest kerfuffle, everyone seemed ready to welcome the newest member of the family, including Graff.

Mrs. Gawne looked down at the cradle that her husband, Alfred, had built for her eighteen years ago. Since then, all of her babies had slept in it.

My, that seems like such a long time ago, she thought. She smiled as she tried to remember each one of them nestled in it next to her. This new little one would do the same for the first few months. Mrs. Gawne like her newborn babes close to her at night, where she could bring them into bed to nurse and slip them back into the cradle to sleep. With that thought, she felt a sense of peace and decided to lay down on the bed and rest a while.

"What *will* you be, little one?" she asked out loud as she placed her hands on her "big tummy," as Myrtle called it. She and her husband had discussed names but couldn't settle on one for a boy. If it were a girl, she would prefer "Bertha." But they would just have to wait and see what the Good Lord would bless them with.

That evening, when the pains began suddenly, Mrs. Gawne sensed that this might be a long labor. She was right, and she suffered through many excruciating hours. A midwife, Mrs. Wade, was sent for early Monday morning, and by noon, the baby was finally born. Mrs. Wade told Mr. Gawne that in all her years, she had never seen a woman suffer so. Mrs. Gawne was exhausted, but eagerly asked to hold her new babe. It seemed to her that the other children had not given her such a hard time. She felt so weak, but it had been worth it when she looked at the precious face of little Bertha.

The happy news traveled to the Bailey home when Graff stopped by to see them Monday evening. Mrs. Bailey decided to "let them be" for a while before visiting, but told Graff to be sure and let them know if anything was needed. Mama told Ethel to wait until tomorrow evening before heading over to the Gawne's home. Ethel was very anxious to go, but agreed to wait, feeling Mama knew best about these matters.

The next evening after supper, Ethel eagerly walked across the field to the Gawne's home carrying some fresh fried cakes.

The children will like these treats, she thought. She was sure the household was very busy with the new arrival, so she was only going to stay a few minutes. Maybe she would be able to take a peek at the new baby. As she approached, she spotted Dr. Miller's horse and buggy pulled up to the house, and then saw Graff on the steps of the front porch, sitting with his head in his hands. Fear gripped Ethel, and she ran the rest of the way.

Breathless, she stopped at Graff's feet. He said through his hands without looking up, "Mama is dead… she's gone."

Ethel was shocked at the news and wondered how this could be true. She sat down beside him on the step and leaned her head on his shoulder. Placing the cakes on the porch, she reached her arm around his back to hold him.

"I'm so sorry," was all she could whisper as Graff's tears turned to sobs. She hung on tightly, as if to hold him together. Ethel had never heard a man cry so hard. She cried too and to hear Graff broke her heart. Suddenly, she heard a child's voice from inside the house call, "Graff."

She felt Graff's shoulders stop shaking, and he raised his head out of his hands. He took his arm and wiped his face across his sleeve as he stood. Ethel, still sitting, silently watched him walk up the stairs to the door. She noticed the back of his shirt was wet from her tears. She reached for a hanky from her skirt pocket and quickly wiped her eyes and nose. Then she could see the children standing together inside the door.

Graff opened the screen door and stepped inside. It creaked shut, and he stood facing his grief-stricken brothers and sisters. Through her tears, Ethel saw the painful expression on Alma's face as she took a step and buried her head in Graff's chest. The others rushed to do the same, and Graff put his strong arms around them. They were all crying and he was comforting them. Beyond them, in back of the house, came the faint sound of a baby's cry. The scene was heartbreaking to Ethel as she stood and watched for a moment.

She spoke without moving, assuming Graff would understand, "I'm going to get my folks." Then she turned and headed toward home as fast as she could run. It was getting dark as she entered the tall weeds in the field. Crying and gasping for breath, her heart racing, and her long skirt dragging against the weeds, she suddenly tripped and fell, landing hard on the ground. It was as if something had just shaken her to the core. She struggled up to her feet again. Standing still for a minute, waiting for her head to stop spinning, the thought came to her that things would never be the same again. In the past few minutes, it seemed that her life had changed forever, but she didn't know how.

She gathered up her skirt and continued to run as images of Mrs. Gawne, her baby, and Graff went through her mind. At last, she reached the path to her house. On she ran through the gate and up the steps to the kitchen door, quickly opening the door and rushing in to tell them the terrible news.

Many days after Mrs. Gawne's death, the family continued to grieve their loss: Mr. Gawne for his wife and companion and the children for their dear mother.

Ethel couldn't forget the sad sight at the funeral of all the children with Graff standing at the grave. The pastor was brief in his words of comfort for the family and ended with reading the words of Jesus:

I am the resurrection, and the life: he that believeth in me, though he were dead, yet shall he live: And whosoever liveth and believeth in me shall never die.

His brothers and sisters were wearing their Sunday best and brave faces that day. Graff, however, looked as though he had the weight of the world on his broad shoulders. Surely, the words of his dear mother's dying request were weighing on him:

"Grafton, look after the children."

And so he did. Graff had so many responsibilities now. He was so busy working the farm and helping raise his brood of siblings that he and Ethel didn't see each other so much, especially in the same way as before.

Graff had changed. No words needed to be spoken of it. He had accepted his new lot in life and would keep his promise to his mother. She, in heaven now, looking down and reminding him,

Greater love hath no man than this, that a man lay down his life for his friends.

And that was what Graff had done. He had laid aside his plans and hopes for his future—*their future*. When Ethel thought of it that way, she was overcome with guilt for being so selfish. She grieved for Graff and his family and saw how hard it was on all of them.

The weeks that followed were the saddest Ethel had ever known. She slipped into a deep despair as she watched the Gawne family suffer, especially the younger children.

Ethel tried to visit them every day, usually with some fresh baked bread, a pie or fried cakes she helped her Mama make. She found these items were very much appreciated since there was no one to fix these special treats for them and they disappeared quickly.

She noticed Alma, just sixteen years old, taking on the tasks her mother had done, and it further saddened Ethel to see her friend's childhood ending so quickly. All the children seemed to have a "lost" look to them. Sometimes there were many hugs and tears between them when she arrived. Ethel tried to comfort them the best she could, but she knew in her heart that their lives were forever scarred by the death of their mother.

Baby Bertha was being cared for by several women. Mrs. Collins was a "wet nurse" who lived nearby and came immediately after Mrs. Gawne's death to feed the baby. Ethel thought the term was strange for someone who shared her body's milk to feed another's child in need. Mrs. Collins would care for Bertha this way until bottles and cow's milk could be arranged. She also showed the girls how to wash and change diapers, bathe the baby, and other ways to care for a little one.

Another woman, Graff's Aunt Mabel, had been coming in to help with the day-to-day meals. She also was dispensing chores that would need to be carried out by all the children when she would no longer be there.

There were several other ladies who stopped by from time to time to bring a welcomed meal or offer to help with the wash, but these visits became fewer and farther between as the weeks went by.

Ethel and her folks were just a stone's throw away if something was needed. Each visit for Ethel was also a time she hoped she would see or talk to Graff.

One day, when Ethel returned to her home from her visit to the Gawne farm, Mrs. Bailey was at the kitchen table kneading bread dough and looked up as her daughter came through the door, walked to her bedroom, and sat on the bed. Ethel's face was downcast, and Mrs. Bailey quickly set the dough to rest, wiped the flour from her hands on her apron, and went to her daughter's side. She sat beside her on the edge of the bed, but Ethel did not look up.

Mrs. Bailey glanced down at the quilt they were sitting on. It was a blend of so many different pieces and colors of fabrics. Some were from her and the girls' old dresses, some from tablecloths and even an old curtain that had hung in the Bailey's bedroom. She had spent many hours cutting out the pieces and then hand-stitching them all together in a colorful checkerboard pattern. It had given her great pleasure to finally lay the finished quilt over her daughters and know that each night, they were covered with it and her love. At times like this, she sometimes longed for those simpler days when her daughter's problems and hurts could be solved with a big kiss and a cookie. But this was not one of those times.

Mrs. Bailey looked at Ethel and took a deep breath. "What's troubling you, dear?" she asked softly.

Ethel didn't even know where to begin. She was a little surprised that Mama had stopped what she was doing and had come to speak to her. She had been miserable for so long now, crying herself to sleep night after night with no one knowing. Now she had a chance to tell someone and no words seemed to come forth.

Instead, with a flood of tears, she buried her face in her hands and sobbed. Mrs. Bailey immediately put her arm around her daughter and hugged her tightly. She let her cry for a few moments and then said to her, "Ethel, you mustn't grieve so. The Lord will see the children are taken care of."

That was only part of it, thought Ethel. She got control of herself and looked into her mother's eyes, which were wet with tears. "Mama, I'm not just feeling sorry for the children. I'm sorry for Graff and myself. It just isn't fair!" She stopped suddenly, even though there was much more to say. She had said those words over and over to herself and God many times. She had wanted everyone to know that *her dreams* had been crushed and *her future happiness* snatched away. But when she finally said them out loud, they sounded very selfish, and she suddenly felt guilty.

Mrs. Bailey had guessed as much. She reached into her apron pocket and pulled out a hanky and handed it to her daughter. After Ethel had wiped her tears and had controlled her crying, Mrs. Bailey continued, "You are being a true friend to Graff in his time of trouble. Do not bear this with so many tears. I want you to try to *smile* to make the load of others a little lighter and not let on to them the burdens you bear. Besides, we cannot know God's will in this matter and may not for many years."

Mrs. Bailey gave her daughter another hug and rose to get back to her bread making. Ethel sat quietly for a few minutes as a sense of peace came over her. She felt humbled by her talk with Mama and decided to take her advice. Most importantly, even though she didn't understand it, she had finally accepted the fact that she and her dear love were on different paths.

All she could do now was continue to be the best friend that Graff needed and pray someday their lives would be joined together again.

Chapter 12
The Old Nest

Sunday, September 25, 1921

After our pleasant visit with our friend, Grafton Gawne, at his dwelling place in Midland, we decided to start for home to reach there in time for dinner. We have enjoyed our time together, especially at the Midland Fairgrounds with the contests, games, and such. It was cool and damp, but we wrapped up well and enjoyed the nice long drive.

We went by way of Bay City and reached home at 1:00 p.m. Lucille soon had a nice warm dinner on the table, which we enjoyed after the long ride home. I found my oldest sister Ret there, and we all spent the time visiting.

Ret, Graff and Ethel

The next day after dinner, Graff headed back to Midland and sister Ret left for Detroit on the morning train.

Sunday, October 16, 1921

It has been a few weeks since Graff's last visit. He drove in last evening to be here to attend church with us. We were all up about 8:30 a.m. to have breakfast and then Graff, Henry, and myself went to the service at the Methodist-Episcopal Church in town. Graff was anxious to hear our new pastor Rev. Reginald R. Feuell preach a sermon. Needless to say, he was not disappointed. We were blessed indeed to have this man of God as our "shepherd." Graff agreed and mentioned kind words to Rev. Feuell as we left.

Reverend R. R. Feuell, Pastor

After the service, I prepared a chicken dinner, which we all enjoyed. About 2:00 p.m., when everyone had finished their apple pie and coffee and the dishes were cleared away and washed, we stepped into the Chevy and went for a drive.

The views of the trees changing colors were splendid to behold. Henry said that they were *at their peak*. It seemed each time we turned a corner, a more glorious view awaited us. After exploring many little side roads, we finally found our way back home.

We had a light lunch and then all headed back to church for the 7:30 p.m. evening service. On our way back home, I asked Graff if he was obliged to leave for his home early in the day on Monday.

He said, "No, I wouldn't have to go for a week, if there was any reason for me to stay. Why do you ask, Ethel, did you want anything?"

"Well, Graff, I'll tell you. Mrs. Jesse Payne and I are the Millington delegates appointed to attend Grand Lodge Rebekah Assembly being held in Lansing. We wanted to go to Saginaw to catch the evening train for Lansing, and the train does not depart until 10:40 p.m. I thought if you did not have to leave for home, perhaps you would not mind staying until after our supper tomorrow and then take us into Saginaw."

"Sure, I'll wait and be glad to take you," he said with a nod.

Many thanks Graff. You are a good old sport.

Monday, October 17, 1921

I called Jesse early in the morning and told her to be ready for us to pick her up at 6:30 p.m. for our ride to Saginaw. She was happy to hear the news and said she would prepare her things for the trip.

After our supper, with traveling bags and umbrella in hand, I bid Henry, Willard, and Lucille good-bye and headed out to the car. We drove uptown and stopped at Jesse's house. She hurried out and got in the backseat with me. Graff turned to see that we were settled in our places and said, "All aboard, ladies, we're on our way."

Jesse and I enjoyed visiting on our drive and it seemed in no time we reached Saginaw. Graff pulled into the train depot, where we checked our baggage and found that we had lots of spare time. So, Graff asked us to attend a movie with him. We accepted the invitation and drove down to the Franklin Theatre.

We certainly enjoyed every minute of our stay at the movie theatre, and the story was so comical. Talk about approaching storms! Wind, rain, and a deluge of water, it just swept everyone off their feet and washed them away into deeper water. Holes were blown in tents, which the ladies tried to stop up with paper, but to no avail and finally men, women, tent, goat, and all were washed away. I'm tickled yet whenever I think of it, and how Graff laughed, too. Poor Jess and I were half sick to pay for our laughter.

Later, we returned to the car and left for the train. We expressed our thanks to our friend for his kind assistance and the pleasant time shown us. *Graff, do you remember how quickly you stopped the car?* Ha ha.

Jess and I purchased our tickets and then visited with Graff until we heard the train approaching and stepped outside with the crowd. Graff carried our traveling bags into the coach and with a warm handclasp and kindly wish that we have a pleasant time during our absence, he said, "Good-bye," lifted his hat and we were left alone.

I will just add a few lines here to say we reached Lansing, going at once to Kern's Hotel and was soon assigned to our room, which proved to be Parlor D, beautifully furnished and with almost everything we needed.

Then Jesse brought forth her lunch, and since it had been several hours since we had eaten, we sat down and enjoyed it immensely.

Thursday, October 20, 1921

After a day of meetings and fellowship with our sister Rebekahs at the Assembly, Jesse left on the train for home. I stayed to travel to Jackson to visit Henry's brother Fred Van Wagnen and wife Madge of 1607 First St., where I had a wonderful visit. While there, I received word from home that my brother Gene was taken ill at Rochester. I immediately wrote Graff to meet me in Saginaw on Saturday if it were possible for him to do so and drive home with me so I would not have to remain in Saginaw till the evening train.

When the train stopped in Saginaw, he was waiting there and took my luggage to the car. Graff, it was at this time that I placed this picture in your hand and you smiled and said, "The best of all."

Ethel, Graff, and Lucille

Then Graff guided the Chevy onto the road and headed back toward Millington.

When we arrived home, I at once got a suitcase packed with the necessary things that I would need in case we found Gene in bed and would have to remain there.

Sunday, October 30, 1921

At about 8:00 a.m., Henry, Lucille, Graff, and I once more stepped into the car and headed for Rochester. Upon our arrival there, we found Gene doing much better and although feeling bad, he was overjoyed at the invitation to take a ride after we had dinner. We drove out several miles with him and saw the city reservoirs.

After the nice, long ride with him, we returned to the Shoe Shop. I made coffee, and we enjoyed a late lunch with him, and then at 4:30 p.m., we had to bid him good-bye and left for home.

We arrived safely at home thanks to our careful driver. We retired unusually early, as all were tired and sleepy after the ride in the cold wind. Lucille decided next time she would wear her winter coat and heavy gloves. It was a wonder she didn't go bareheaded.

Henry had his overcoat but had forgotten to take a neck scarf. When we discovered he had his red bandana handkerchief tied around his neck and he caught us laughing, when we looked again he had taken it off. Oh dear, I laugh yet when I think how comical he looked.

The others often smile when they see me come out with my big blanket shawl on my arm, but I don't feel bad for if I begin to feel cold, then I'm glad to have it with me. I know the others can stand the cold better than I can, and I believe in going prepared for a change in the weather. Little did we know that in a few weeks, Graff would solve the problem of cold and windy rides with him.

Friday, November 18, 1921

At 6:20 p.m., we heard the sound of auto wheels and upon going to the back door, we discovered Graff had driven in with his new Ford sedan. It is a beautiful machine and has plenty of room for passengers. Best of all, it is enclosed with windows, which I know will make for pleasant viewing and warmth as we travel along. *Well done, Laddie!*

We all celebrated his dandy purchase with a hot supper and then attended a play at the Opera House in the evening put on by Millington High School.

Saturday, November 19, 1921

We spent the day working, visiting, etc. Henry got home from working at the mill at 5:00 p.m., and we had an early supper. Then Our Four started out for Flint in the new machine to attend the movie *The Adventures of Tarzan*, which we all enjoyed.

Upon reaching home at 11:50 p.m., Henry and Graff went to the barn with the car. Lucille and I entered the house and found a cap and overcoat hanging on the hall tree. We looked into the south bedroom and found that empty, so I went upstairs to see who was in bed with Willard. When lo, I beheld a man sleeping in my bed! I went over to the bed and looked over carefully and found it was my brother Gene from Rochester, so I looked for a place elsewhere to sleep.

Sunday, November 20, 1921

We stayed home from church this morning and visited with our company. Later on, after our dinner, I fixed up a plate of food for Mrs. Wildfong, and we started out for our usual drive, stopping long enough for Gene to call on Mrs. Wildfong. Then we went on by way of Vassar, Tuscola, Elkhorn, and home. The drive and visit were a great treat for brother Gene.

Monday, November 21, 1921

Graff told Gene if he could wait until tomorrow, he was going to drive through to Detroit and would take him back to Rochester. Gene consented to wait and enjoy the ride back with him by auto.

I asked, "Why can't I go along and visit sister Ret and ride back?"

Graff said, "You know you are always welcome. There is lots of room, and I'll take you there and call for you when I'm ready to come back."

So I hustled into the work, did some baking, and got things ready for Lucille to get the meals during my absence.

After supper, Henry went to join the Masons at the Millington Lodge. He had been a member of the International Order of Odd Fellows for some time, and several of the lodge brothers persuaded him to unite with them also.

Tuesday, November 22, 1921

At 7:53 a.m., Graff, Gene, and I left for Rochester, via Otisville, around the lake, on through Columbiaville and into Lapeer at 9:10 a.m.

Graff stopped at a garage for some gas. Upon leaving Lapeer, we followed the Blue and Gold sign and on through Hunters Creek until we heard the sound of an explosion. I called out, "What's that?"

Graff replied, "Blowout!" Yes, it was; and that's where we all got out of the car. And very good naturedly, Gene and I stepped out and the boys investigated. Graff said, "Gene, bring on the new tire from the rear."

He obeyed at once and said, "Nothing like being prepared."

While the boys were changing the tire, I went over to the yard by us and visited with a lady at her pantry window. I discovered later that I lost my handkerchief on my way back to the car. All was in shape again; only the boys' hands are pretty dirty from changing the tire. But they refused the clean towel I offered them from my traveling bag. So we stepped into the Ford and moved briskly away at 9:48 a.m.

We had a short stop at Metamora, where Graff went into a store and bought some bananas, and they certainly were fine. Gene said, "Those are just ripe enough to eat. I'll take another and not let them get too ripe." Ha ha.

We finally hit pavement at 11:15 a.m. Graff pulled up to the Shoe Repair Shop, and we all got out. Gene unlocked the door, and we went inside where I took off my wraps and lit the oil stove to put the tea kettle on. Graff then went to the market for meat while I went to the bakery for bread, fried cakes, cookies, cheese, and butter. We soon sat down and enjoyed our dinner.

We visited until 2:30 p.m. when we said good-bye to Gene, stepped into the car, and headed for Detroit. Soon we arrived at the corner of Dix and Military, turned the corner, and halted at 6120 Dix Ave. I rang the bell and mounted the stairs. The door opened and Mae stood there wide-eyed and exclaimed, "Why, it's Aunt Ethel and Graff! Come in." Poor Ret was so glad to see us she could hardly talk.

Twas 4:25 p.m. when Graff said, "I must soon go out and phone my sister Bertha and have Herman come after me, for I don't know where to find them." So he went down to the drugstore and phoned them. He then came back and waited for Herman to arrive. Soon Herman drove up and Graff got into his car and followed him back to their place where he will spend the night.

Wednesday, November 23, 1921

Graff and his "baby" sister Bertha came over and all were determined that we stay over for Thanksgiving. It was left to me to decide. Graff said, "Ethel, if you think Henry will worry if you don't get back Thursday, we will go home."

I said, "I told him before I left home, if Ret and Mae did not have other company and wanted me to stay over, I would do so." They all seemed pleased with my decision to stay. Graff and Bertha then left to go back to her place, while I stayed with Ret and Mae to visit and helped them prepare for the next day's Thanksgiving meal.

Thursday, November 24, 1921
Thanksgiving Day

O give thanks unto the Lord, for he is good:
for his mercy endureth forever.

We girls had a good day together and later, Mae had insisted that Graff come over and have six o'clock Thanksgiving dinner with our bunch and help us eat the chicken and all the other good things she prepared. He came late in the evening, and we all did eat.

At 10:00 p.m., Bertha and Herman came by to visit and had us come back with them. As she had invited me to spend the night with her, good-byes were said to Ret and Mae. We gathered up my belongings and went down to where the cars were parked. Herman and Bertha moved out, and Graff followed quickly to keep them in sight.

We reached Bertha's about 11:30 p.m. She had a baked goose in the oven, baked potatoes, brown gravy, salad, and so forth, and we ate again. *We all certainly had plenty of food to be thankful for this day.*

Then we had to sit up and visit, for it is not good for one's health to eat and then retire immediately after, so we stayed up until 2:45 a.m. Graff and Herman crept away into their bedroom, and Bertha and I took the front bedroom and were soon asleep. But oh, that little dog! I'd ring its neck, if it were mine unless I could make it quit barking and waking everybody up in the house.

Friday, November 25, 1921

We were all up at 10:00 a.m. and had breakfast. Shortly after, all was in readiness for the homeward drive. Good-byes were said and on we went, reaching Rochester and the little Shoe Shop at 1:20 p.m. We went in and had dinner with brother Gene. We visited until 3:00 p.m., when once more we had to bid him good-bye and leave him alone. *Poor fellow. His is a lonely life too since the death of his wife.*

On we traveled, reaching Lapeer at 5:00 p.m. *Drive slower, old boy, and don't run over those cows wandering through.* The road was clear at last, and we sped up just as a big dog jumped from the gateway and chased two cows in front of the car. Only that the big fellow was quick at the wheel did we avoid a catastrophe. Whew!

Finally, we reached our Millington home safe and sound. We found that Henry and Lucille were surprised to see us. Henry said, "By Jove, I didn't look for you till tomorrow. Did you have a good visit with the folks?"

Well, if you could have heard Ret and I until two o'clock in the morning, you would know we did not go to sleep on the job, until Mae came in and said, "Don't you folks know the rest of us would like to get to sleep before daylight?"

Henry laughed and said, "I'm glad you went, for they visit just that way here Graff, every time Ret and her get together."

Well, I can't help it. I think of something else every little while and unless I say it then, I might forget it. We three visited until 10:30 p.m. Then, as all were tired, we said good-night and went to bed.

Sunday, November 27, 1921

Our youngest daughter, Lucille, is twenty-two years old today.

I decided to prepare her favorite meal today to celebrate. So, after church, we were just ready to sit down to dinner when Graff drove in. He joined us as we enjoyed roast beef, potatoes and gravy, cooked carrots, honey buns, dill pickles, and pumpkin pie. My, we did eat, especially Lucille.

Friday, December 9, 1921

Two weeks later, Graff drove in at 7:00 p.m., and we all enjoyed the evening. Henry had told me to write and tell Graff he had better come prepared to take me over to Davison and get my teeth. So, he inquired if I was going for them tomorrow. I said, "Yes, if you care to drive there with me."

He said, "Sure, I'll take you. It would be a pleasure to go if it was as far as Chicago." Ha ha. I guess they were anxious for me to get my new teeth.

Saturday, December 10, 1921

We were all up and hurried to get ready to go to Davison. I invited Thalia to bring Theo and Billy and come with us. She gladly accepted, and we soon were on our way. We reached the office of Dr. Harrison, and I went in and he waited on me almost immediately. Then I went downstairs and called for Graff. He went up, was introduced, and the doctor drained three teeth for him. We then all entered the Ford and hurried home. The children enjoyed their little trip and talked all the way there and back.

That evening, after our supper, Graff drove Lucille, Thalia, and me into Flint to a movie show. We all enjoyed a good time, and Thalia and I seemed to see the funny side of everything and almost laughed our heads off.

Sunday, December 11, 1921

We all went to church and after our dinner drove out to Watrousville. We stopped on our way to see how Mrs. John Lovejoy was doing after her long illness and found that she was dying. Our call was a brief one, and we returned to the car and went on our way. As we rode in silence, the closing words of Rev. Feuell came back to my mind.

To everything there is a season, and a time to every purpose under the heaven: A time to be born, and a time to die;

It appears Mrs. Lovejoy's "time" is very near. *God bless her in her final hours here on earth. She will be dearly missed.*

Lucille was driving for Graff this day, and soon we found that we had struck a hole that required the help of both men to get us out. *Did you ask if there was any mud?* Ask Graff, and he will answer the question. He was just wearing a new suit of clothes. After removing the car from the mudhole, my oh my, he was a dirty-looking boy.

Monday, December 12, 1921

We just put in the time visiting, then after dinner, Graff said, "Ethel, I must start for home as I want to stop in Saginaw and take a man to the farm at Midland and try to sell him one of my horses."

Twas 2:00 p.m., and I watched him as he moved around the house and got his coats and traveling bag ready to go. I realized how lonely his life was when he went out and away to that far away lonesome home. I thought how much sadness that is in life that not many others ever know. As our friends and loved ones go about their daily tasks, perhaps with a smile on their faces, yet the heart is too full for words.

And so Graff said good-bye, stepped out the back door, and headed to the east end of the house, and on into the next yard where the Sedan was parked. After putting his bags in, he looked back, lifted his hat, and was gone.

That evening about 8:30 p.m., I was sitting beside the stove with my blanket shawl wrapped around me when the telephone rang. Lucille called, "Answer it, Mama."

So I got up, took down the receiver and said, "Hello?"

Central operator said, "Just a minute for Saginaw."

Soon the big laddie was on the line and said, "Ethel, that you? Well, I've been to Midland with my man, sold my horse, got back with the man to Saginaw, and had my supper. Thought you would like to know that everything is okay."

You're a *thoughtful boy,* and you know I'm always glad to hear from you and of your success in everything that is right and for your good.

Sunday, December 18, 1921

About 10:15 a.m., the telephone rang and I answered, and it was this laddie calling up. "Graff, you sound so close by. Where are you?"

He laughed and said, "I'm over at Mayville. Stayed here last night, and I am now ready to leave but wanted to know how you are this morning."

"Not sick in bed but sitting beside the stove in the big rocking chair and wrapped up in my big woolen shawl. Feeling too bad to go out to church, but some better than I was the day you went home. Thanks for your kindly remembrance."

It often does as much good as a dose of medicine to know our friends remember us and take the pains to call up when far away and inquire how we are. And I want you to always remember, Graff, that no matter where you are, you can't go so far but what I shall always think of you and the many happy hours we've spent together.

Friday, December 23, 1921

At 6:30 p.m., Graff drove in to attend the Encampment No. 64 IOOF to be held at the opera house. The degree team from Lapeer initiated about forty members. Then they all came to the IOOF Hall where ten Rebekah Sisters dressed in white and wearing pink and white caps, waited on them and served a bountiful supper. Grand Patriarch Houck of Detroit made a motion that the brothers take up a collection for the Flower Fund for the ladies, and we realized $13.61. *Thank you.* We reached home about 12:30 a.m., and all retired.

Saturday, December 24, 1921

All up early and we had our breakfast. I got the big goose that Graff brought on to parboil before we started for Davison, for my new teeth need filing. I'm getting old. Ha ha. Graff got me to the office of Dr. Harrison, and he was not long in finding where the trouble was. In less than ten minutes, he had my teeth fixed, and we were on our way home.

I hurried and cooked dinner, for Graff was expecting Rev. R. R. Feuell to come by and visit for an hour with him. Sure enough, he arrived on time at 12:30 p.m. While they visited, and all afternoon I was busy getting the Christmas tree in readiness and preparing the Christmas supper.

For good reasons, we observed today, Saturday, December 24 as Christmas. Graff drove down to Father and Mother Van's house and brought them back to us.

Father and Mother Van

Father Van brought his Bible and favored us with a reading.

And the angel said unto them, Fear not: for behold, I bring you good tidings of great joy, which shall be to all people. For unto you is born this day in the city of David a Savior, which is Christ the Lord. And this shall be a sign unto you; Ye shall find the babe wrapped in swaddling clothes, lying in a manger. And suddenly there was with the angel a multitude of the heavenly host praising God, and saying, Glory to God in the highest, and on earth peace, good will toward men. (Luke 2:10–14)

Father Van slowly closed his well-worn Bible, and many in our company responded with a heartfelt "Amen." The reading certainly blessed all who heard it.

At 6:30 p.m., the goose and all the trimmings were ready to enjoy. We found our places at the dining room table. I had set in two extra leaves to be able to seat our large gathering. There was Father and Mother Van, who took their places at the end of the table. Next came Graff, our son John and his wife Maybelle, our daughter Thalia and her family, husband Vilas and their children Little Theo and Billy. Then came daughter Lucille and son Willard. Henry and I finished the number and found our places at the other end of the long table. We enjoyed our Christmas meal and our company immensely, finished off with mince pie.

Thirteen gathered together—an unlucky number some would say, but I was thankful that God had spared those dear ones and felt we were lucky to have them all well and able to meet with us on the Christmas of 1921.

This was the first time we have had all our family home on this date since our soldier boys returned from overseas.

Vilas and John
"Home from Over There"

This picture always looks good to me. It was taken the day we met John at Flint for the first time after his return from France.

Sunday, December 25, 1921
Christmas Day

We spent a much quieter day than yesterday, visiting and eating off the leftovers from our Christmas feast. After dinner, Graff said, "Where do you want to go?"

I said, "I'd like to go to Clio and call on some dear friends there and leave my Christmas gift for them. It's the pictures that were taken this past summer, which I'm quite sure they will enjoy."

"All right, let's go." So Graff, Henry, and I left at once and called at the home of Sina and Orkie Hempstead, where I was warmly welcomed by them, and also by Grandma Atwood and Laura. And last but not least, by Billy, who, like the others, was glad to see me. We have been friends for years.

Billy

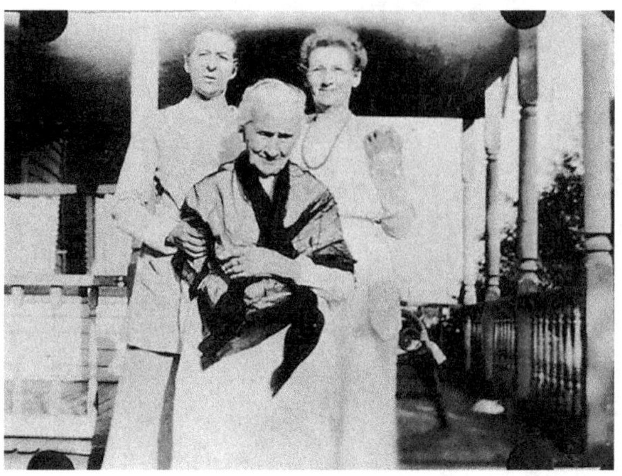

Laura, Grandma Atwood, and Ethel

(Sad note: Eight months after this visit, on August 26, 1922, Billy shot himself in his room at the Bryant Hotel in Flint, Michigan.)

After we returned home, we had a light lunch and attended the 7:30 p.m. Christmas service at church. It was a fine service, which ended with the singing of the beloved hymn:

Silent Night, holy night,
All is calm, all is bright,
Round yon virgin mother and child,
Holy infant so tender and mild.
Sleep in heavenly peace,
Sleep in heavenly peace.

By the time the congregation ended with the fourth verse, our Christmas was complete with the words:

Silent night, holy night,
Son of God, love's pure light.
Radiant beams from Thy holy face,
with the dawn of redeeming grace.

Jesus, Lord at Thy birth;
Jesus, Lord at Thy birth.

Monday, December 26, 1921

No signs of the washwoman around our kitchen today. We visited through the day and when Henry got home at 5:00 p.m. from the mill, we planned to drive to Flint and attend the theatre. So immediately after supper, we left and arrived at downtown Flint, parked the car, and went to see the movie play, *The Old Nest.*

It certainly was fine and portrayed the patient, long-suffering, never ending love of a woman—a mother's love. Not until her children have been absent perhaps for many years and return to find her golden locks turned to gray do they find her with the same loving hands outstretched, eager to clasp them to her breast. Not till then do they realize how steadfast and true she has been.

We felt doubly paid for our trip and reached home feeling fine and retired about midnight.

Tuesday, December 27, 1921

We had the usual breakfast and then sat down and visited until 11:00 a.m. Graff prepared to get started for home, feeling he certainly had enjoyed the past five days immensely. He expressed the wish that we might all live to be as happy and see as pleasant a year in 1922 as this the year of 1921 has been.

Graff left at 11:15 a.m. and backed the Ford Sedan out from the south side of the house where it stood. I watched him as he turned the car onto the highway and passed from view.

Thus ended the happy year of 1921.

Chapter 13
Whiskers

Looking Back to the 1880s

The Bailey Farm—Fall 1891

One evening in mid-October, after supper and cleaning up the kitchen for her mother, Ethel slipped out the front door and slowly made her way from her home through the field to the nearby bridge. This little wooden bridge near the Gawne farm was the place of many pleasant memories for her. She breathed in the cool, crisp air and gazed at the trees surrounding her. The beauty of the fall colors was a favorite of hers, and she loved this time of the changing seasons. The golden yellow and orange leaves of the maples, deep rusty oaks, and bright crimson sumac bushes all seemed to glow in the setting sunlight. The sky was streaked with rose and violet-colored clouds, and Ethel was in awe of the beauty on display.

She reached the bridge and slowly walked on and stood holding the iron railing. It was so peaceful, and she longed to share this glorious scene of "*God's handiwork*" with someone. She thought of the many times she and Graff had found themselves there to enjoy the sparkling water in the creek below and smiled as she remembered the times they stood there; sometimes quietly enjoying the natural beauty, other times talking of their future. She had always known in her heart that their future would be together. But alas, now she stood on this bridge alone, with just the sound of the leaves rustling in the trees and the whip-poor-will singing in the distance.

Even though she was only seventeen, Ethel suddenly felt old and strangely sad as she pictured herself and Graff laughing and running hand in hand through the field on their way to the bridge.

"What has happened to all those wonderful, carefree days?" she asked herself. No matter what the future held, she would always look back to those days as the happiest in her life. Nothing, she thought, would ever compare to them. *Why do things have to change?*

"Enough of this feeling sorry for yourself, Ethel Bailey," she reminded herself. After all, hadn't she just said those words in church this past Sunday? "Thy Kingdom come, Thy will be done..." Even though she didn't understand, it had been good for her to pray, and afterward, she had felt at peace.

She watched as a yellow leaf fell from a nearby tree and slowly drifted down to land on the water. Her thoughts turned back to days gone by as one particular happy time came to mind. She closed her eyes and recalled those precious moments again...

It had begun as she was on her way to the Gawne farm because Graff had mentioned something to her the night before when he visited. He said he wanted to show her something but wouldn't tell her what it was no matter how much she pleaded. When she arrived bright and early the next morning, Graff was over by the barn, standing by the gate looking into the horse yard. She had waved, quickened her pace, and was a little out of breath when she got to the gate where Graff greeted her. He told her to climb the old wooden fence and sit on top for a good view. She wondered what he was up to. After all, she had seen these horses many times, and nothing about them looked unusual to her.

Still, she did as Graff requested and climbed up carefully so as not to catch her foot on her skirt. Settling down on the gate with her hands in her lap, she looked at him still standing below her. "Well, what is it?" she insisted.

"My, you look very grand up there," he said with a grin, as he seemed pleased with his little joke. He liked to tease her sometimes, just for his own amusement.

"Graff," she shot back, "you help me down this minute!" She tried to act stern, but it wasn't working, and she had to purse her lips tightly to keep from laughing.

He reached up and put his strong hands around her waist and quickly lifted her up off the fence and unexpectedly held her up over his head. He laughed, and she let out a scream of excitement before he lowered her and set her down gently on the ground saying, "You're light as a feather." He was still grinning as he stood there with his hands on his hips.

"And you are *crazy,* Laddie!" They both burst into laughter as Graff grabbed her hand and started for the barn. "Come on, you'll really want to see this."

She didn't protest because she could tell this time Graff really did have something to show her. They reached the barn door, went in, and turned to the right toward the corner. That's when she spotted a small makeshift bedding area, and as they got closer, she could see a cat lying in the bed of straw on the floor, and in front of her were her newborn kittens.

"Oh, Graff, when did she have them?" she asked as they drew near.

"Early yesterday morning, as near as I can figure," he said as he knelt down beside them. She followed his lead and knelt quietly beside him, not wanting to disturb the new little family. She noticed the two boards that were pressed up next to the bed of straw. *Graff must have put the boards there to "fence them in" and keep the kittens from wandering out.* But, of course, right now they couldn't get into much trouble.

The mother cat was resting quietly but was keeping busy with the wiggling and mewing new family. She was licking tops of heads, tails, and everything in between as she lovingly tended to each one.

"How many does she have?" she'd asked as she counted heads. "Four?"

"Five," Graff replied as one popped out from underneath the rest. It had been buried by the others but not for long. Turning to her, he said, "You have first choice, remember?"

She nodded as she carefully reached in and touched the mother cat on the head to reassure her. She didn't touch any of the kittens on this first visit but planned to keep a close watch as they grew in the next few weeks. The kittens were all different colors. One was identical to its mother with calico markings. The rest were an assortment of gray and white. They were all so cute that she was going to have a hard time choosing one.

Ethel made many visits to the barn as the weeks went by. Sometimes, the other children were there with her holding the kittens and watching them eat and play. They all took notice of how fast they were growing, and some of the children were beginning to have favorites. But Graff had already told all his brothers and sisters that Ethel would have first choice of a kitten. They were all fine with that since Ethel was like an older sister to them. They loved her as such and willingly let her decide on the fuzzy gray male with the white feet. Graff had already checked the kittens out and told her, "That's a tom."

At last, the day came when the kittens were old enough to be on their own. She had come to the Gawne farm that day carrying a piece of cloth retrieved from a drawer where Mama kept rags. She went into the barn and heard the familiar sound of meowing kittens. Graff followed her in and watched as she picked up the kitten and held him to his mother's face. The cat licked him good-bye, and she wrapped him snugly in the cloth, making sure his little head was sticking out.

Graff had walked them home that day, and on their way, she told him that she had named the kitten *Whiskers*. "That's a funny name for an old tomcat that is going to spend most of his time catching mice," he'd said, amused.

Ethel knew Whiskers would catch his share of mice to earn his keep, but she planned on making him her special pet and spoiling him with lots of attention. She would treat him to table scraps and figured Papa would soon be slipping him tidbits under the table during dinner.

As time went by, Whiskers grew from a playful kitten into a plump and healthy cat. He was just right for petting while lying on one's lap and unbeknownst to her folks; sometimes he crept quietly into Ethel's room at night and curled up to sleep on her bed. He became her companion to share many of her thoughts and dreams and even some heartaches. He gave her comfort many times by just being there for her to pet and tell her secrets to.

As Ethel recalled these memories, she felt something brushing against her skirt at her feet that suddenly brought her thoughts back to the present. Looking down, she saw Whiskers with his back arched, leaning into her leg. She reached down and picked him up in both arms and pressed her cheek to the top of his head. The cat contently nuzzled her in return and began to purr loudly. She held him close and stroked his soft fur for a few moments before whispering in his ear, "Let's go home."

It was getting dark now, but Ethel would have no problem finding her way home. The sound of her steps on the wooden bridge turned to the quiet rustling of her shoes in the grass as she slowly walked back toward home, still holding her companion; she prayed that God would grant her a brighter tomorrow.

Chapter 14
New Friend

January 1922—A Happy New Year Grafton!

May the New Year be a happy one with just as many pleasant days for you as the past year has held.

May your life be sweeter and better for you having been permitted to live and enjoy the year that has just ended.

May God direct you, so your feet will lead you into paths of blessings and ways of peace.

And when each day is spent and the twilight shadows fall, and you sit and ponder, may the feeling of sweet rest and peace come to you in this thought:

I've done my best.

Wednesday, January 5, 1922

On this date, a postcard was mailed from Rose City to me, and on it were these words:

> *"Dear Friends,*
> *On our way for the hunt. Have to leave car here and drive 14 miles with team of horses. Expect to leave in a few minutes. Hope everybody is well. Write me at Rose City and I will get my mail here.*
> *Graff"*

Once more showing that although he was on his way with his men friends for a good time, he did not forget the friends he had left behind. They did have a good time and some experience with cold and knee-deep snow. Then, finally, after it showed signs of a harder storm approaching, they rolled up their belongings and on Saturday, January 14, they returned to Midland.

Friday, January 27, 1922

Henry came in from the mill shortly after 5:00 p.m., and we were visiting beside the hard coal stove when we heard a rap at the back door.

I said to him, "Someone is at the door. Go and see who it is."

Henry left and soon I heard him speaking to someone. Immediately, he came back in and said, "There is a man out there, and he wonders if you will let him stay the night."

Without getting out of my chair to investigate the case, a thought struck me and I said, "Yes, bring him in. He can have his supper and a warm bed to sleep in." And upon rising to my feet and starting for the kitchen, I saw the face and form of our dear friend partly hidden behind Henry.

Both boys laughed and asked how I ventured to say yes before I knew who was out there. I left them to guess, and I shook hands with Graff and passed into the kitchen and prepared supper for ourselves and the always welcome "tramp."

Saturday, January 28, 1922

Henry worked at the mill today, so at 5:00 p.m., Graff drove uptown and brought him home. After supper, it was decided that we would attend a movie at the Fenton Hall Movie Theatre in downtown Flint. Here you see a nice postcard picture of the inside of the structure where we have spent many enjoyable and entertaining visits.

Sunday, January 29, 1922

We attended church services this morning, and we had dinner a little earlier than usual. The boys planned to go for a ride, so Henry was trying to hurry me away from the table. I got up when the front door opened and son John and wife Maybelle came in. I asked if they had been to dinner.

Maybelle said, "No, we came *down here* for dinner." Ha ha. So I prepared a place for them.

While they were eating, we invited them to go for a ride with us. They accepted and soon Graff and John took the front seat; Maybelle, Henry, and I the back and away we go to the corner. Turning east going over the "Hills" to North Lake and on to Otter Lake, past where the new brick schoolhouse had recently burned. Then we headed for home. Maybelle enjoyed the trip too, for she had never been over to the lakes.

Monday, January 30, 1922

Somehow, the washwoman fails to be on duty on certain Mondays, and as this was her day off, of course, there is no washing done. We just put in the time visiting until 4:30 p.m. when Graff left for Vassar.

Monday, February 13, 1922

Two weeks later in the evening, the telephone rang just as we were sitting down to dinner. Willard answered, but he couldn't understand what the central operator wanted, so he called to me. I answered, and it was Graff. He was at his sister Ollie's home in Vassar. She had informed him she wanted him to drive her and sister Laura to Detroit to see their "baby" sister Bertha who had been quite sick.

Graff said, "The girls want you and Henry to come along with us, and you can visit your sister Ret." I told him we would be ready for him when he came along to pick us up.

But, as Chas Garner had lost his nice home and contents by fire the night before, Henry hesitated and said, "I feel afraid of the fires, but you go if you want. I will stay here." So, I too thought I would stay home.

But when Graff drove up and the girls came in and urged me so hard to go with them, I told them I would be right with them.

Ollie said, "Hurry up and get ready to go with us! You don't get a chance like this very often, to be taken and brought back. We will all have a better time, and none of us will have to sit alone."

So I dressed quickly, put a few articles into my traveling bag, and the four of us stepped into the car. At 2:00 p.m., we started on our journey southward.

At 3:20 p.m., Ollie and I complained of cold feet and thought we would take the robe we were sitting on and put it over our laps. She attempted to raise the traveling bag and in doing so, tried to *hang me* feet first. We laughed till our sides ached.

We reached Rochester at 4:35 p.m. where we stopped at A.E. Bailey Shoe Shop. We all went in and visited for a few minutes with my brother Gene. He was glad to see us, even for a short time. A few minutes later, good-byes were said, and we reentered the car and on we traveled toward Detroit.

We arrived at the home of Mr. and Mrs. Herman Koch at 7749 Hendria Avenue at 6:00 p.m. All of us drew a breath of relief as we stepped out on the ground, glad to know we were safe after the long ride in heavy traffic. Our driver did fine not hitting anyone and moving quickly enough so that a truck didn't hit us.

We found Herman just leaving the front porch to catch a streetcar to go to work at the theatre. He greeted us and gave us a hearty welcome and then hurried on to his work. We entered the house and found Bertha feeling lots better. With her was Zella Gawne of Saginaw—Graff's brother's wife. We soon got supper ready, which we all enjoyed.

After visiting until quite a late hour when we began to feel we couldn't keep our eyes open much longer, we planned just *how* we were all going to sleep. There were five ladies, Herman and Graff and only two beds and a davenport. We decided that Zella, Laura, and I would occupy the widest bed in the parlor bedroom. Ollie and Bertha would take the davenport in the parlor, and the "boys" would share the bed in the other bedroom.

Laura prepared for bed and was the first one in, so she took the back of the bed. I answered to number two at roll call, and I lay in the middle.

Then last but not least came Zella, but we were all too tired to be anything but good-natured and in a short time, we fell asleep.

Tuesday, February 14, 1922

The morning found us all there, and maybe we had to add an extra tint of pink to our cheeks to make us look just right. Anyhow, we were able to be up and ate our breakfast at 9:00 a.m. Shortly after, Herman said he would ride over with Graff and show him the way so he could take me to Ret's house.

We got started at last and reached 6120 Dix Avenue at 11:45 a.m. and found Ret sick in bed. She had been there for three days, and Mae had a lame back and could hardly walk. Mae sat up and visited with Herman and Graff, and I went to Ret's bedroom to see her. She was so glad I had come that she cried.

The boys soon left for the theatre, and we three women were left alone. We got our lunch and about 4:30 p.m., we went into Ret's room and found her dressing.

She said, "Ethel, you needn't think I'm going to stay in bed while you are here. Your visit will do me more good than the medicine the doctor left."

Mae prepared a veal and pork dish called "A la king" for our supper, and how we all did eat. *I wish I had a dish of it right now.*

At 12:30 a.m., we all retired, but Ret and I visited until 2:45 a.m. There was likely to be a scolding in store for us unless we quit, so we said good-night.

Wednesday, February 15, 1922

Ret and I were up at 10:30 a.m. and made toast and coffee. At 1:00 p.m., Graff, Bertha, and Zella came over for me. We said our good-byes to Ret and Mae and returned to 7749 Hendria Avenue. We had our lunch at 3:20 p.m., then left Herman's front porch, and went out to the car. Laura and Ollie insisted I ride with the driver on the return trip, so we stepped one by one, waved farewell, and were on our way toward Rochester.

We reached there at 4:20 p.m. and found Gene had a nice fresh custard pie being delivered and insisted on our helping him eat it. I sent the little girl back to get another. We all got out of the car and went in and enjoyed the pie and a few minutes visiting with Gene. At 4:45 p.m., we were on the road again.

We reached my home in Millington at 7:07 p.m. *I see Henry kept the house from burning down.* We arrived, and we girls were not very cold or tired. Only Graff's hands were cold, so he was glad to warm them over the kitchen fire while I hurriedly made some hot tea for him and the girls to drink. Then, Graff and the girls left for Vassar, thus ending a pleasant little trip, which we will not forget.

Thursday, March 2, 1922

I was taken sick with heart trouble, followed by the "flu." It kept me pretty close to the couch or bed for many days. A week later, on Friday evening, I sat in the big rocker beside the coal fire. As I enjoyed the warmth, I found myself staring at the pretty shamrock design on the stove.

Suddenly, the front door opened and Graff stepped in. It was like the coming of a thunderbolt out of a clear sky. The surprise sight of him almost left me speechless. I managed to ask, "Why, Graff, how did you come?"

He laughed and said, "With the car, but it is stuck in the mud out here by the upper driveway." Henry and Vilas helped him out, and he then took the car to the parking garage uptown.

Saturday, March 11, 1922

We had a nice visit and then all went to the mill and got weighed. I found my illness was *no sham,* for I had been weighing 140 pounds, but today when I stepped on the scales, they scarcely balanced 130 pounds. You could see I had failed, "But now, I'm satisfied that you all realize as never before how *much* I had failed in the past few weeks!"

After supper, Graff decided to drive up to Vassar and stay overnight with his sister Ollie. So about 7:00 p.m., he took Henry out to help him start the car. After "striking her off," Henry got in and Graff drove him to Mr. Sherwood's to get eggs to set a hen. I stood by the front window and watched them as they drove away.

After they were gone, I went into the bedroom to lay down, but soon heard the sound of the car returning and both boys came in. I was surprised, but Graff said, "Why, Ethel, you didn't think I'd gone home without say good-bye, did you?"

I said, "I thought you had forgotten."

He said, "No, I don't forget. But now, I'll just say good-night, Ethel, for I'm coming back down tomorrow and will take you and Henry for a ride, for I think the drive will do you good if we don't travel far enough to tire you." Then he stepped out and into the car and left us alone once more.

Sunday, March 12, 1922

The next day, Henry went to church in the morning, but I was not well enough, so I remained at home and got dinner ready. Graff drove in just as Henry returned from Sunday school at 1:00 p.m. We ate dinner, and I suggested we drive to Otisville and see Henry's sister Kate and husband Claude Phipps who was ill with rheumatism. I fixed a nice box of fruit for him and soon we were out to the car ready to start. Graff and Henry occupied the front seat, and I took the back.

Upon our arrival at the home in Otisville, we found a couple of cars there ahead of us. Graff said he would wait for us, so Henry and I left him and went into the house for a few minutes. On our return, Henry said, "How will we ride going back?"

Graff said, "Ethel, better take the easiest place." So I took the front seat and wrapped my blanket over my legs. *Thank you.*

Strange, but most of the time, the front seat is given to me. For my dearest friends have come to know that it is the easiest place to ride, and they must think the best is none too good for me. Even Henry's brother Fred of Jackson will take his place at the wheel and say, "Come on, my dear sister, and take your place beside me."

We headed back by way of Henpeck and arrived home safely. Although very weak and tired, I enjoyed the ride and felt it did me more good than staying at home would have done. Thank you, dear thoughtful friend "for my flowers." We spent the evening at home, had a late lunch as usual, and finally all retired.

Monday, March 13, 1922

Had our breakfast and while Henry went to the mill, Graff and I discussed the many visits and pleasant drives we've taken together during the past year. Surely, we can look back and feel it has been one of the happiest years we have ever known. *Twelve months,* and during that time, seldom has more than two weeks passed that we have not all been together. At 10:45 a.m., Graff said good-bye and left for his home in Midland.

Tuesday, March 14, 1922

One year ago, tonight, Graff entered our home sad-eyed, thin and pale, looking as though he had no hope or aim in life and only weighing 197 pounds. When he was weighed at the mill last Saturday, he tipped the scales to just 227 pounds. It seems that all the good food and loving company this past year has surely helped him. And best of all, the return of that grand old smile to his face.

Graff, have you ever been sorry you came? "No, never," was his reply.

March 21, 1922

Dear Old Book,

Many things have happened to sadden me since I wrote on your pages last, and it seems as though today my heart is too sad and full to even try to write. *But I know that unless I do, no one else will finish these pages.*

Just now, I feel I would like to steal out and far away from work and friends and have just a few hours all to myself. But, as that privilege is even denied me, I will not murmur but will pick up the broken threads and continue with my daily tasks.

I'm thinking of our vacation and fishing trip, how since June 1921 we have looked forward to 1922.

But somehow today I feel that if we go, the happiness and pleasure will not be the same. For I have a feeling that something is going to happen in some way; that dark clouds will hover over us, where before was all sunshine and happiness.

Friday, March 24, 1922

At 6:20 p.m., Graff drove in to attend our play put on by the Community Club members, entitled "The Podunk Limited." We all enjoyed seeing many of our friends in the play and had many good laughs besides. Lucille joined us as she was home after working for a few months at a factory in Detroit. She was making a good amount while there, but she said it was not for her. She had been staying in a large hotel with all the other women who worked there. Tis good to have her home.

After the play, we came home and had some chocolate cake and hot tea. We visited awhile and then retired early; all agreeing that we could use the rest.

Saturday, March 25, 1922

All up at the usual hour and had breakfast. After eating, we visited a while since Graff's stay would be a short one. At 11:20 a.m., Graff walked up to the "Ten-Cent Barn" to get his car. He bid us good-bye and headed on to his Midland home.

Before leaving, he said, "Henry, don't fail to be in Saginaw Tuesday eve at the Masonic Lodge, and I'll be there to meet you."

Tuesday, March 28, 1922

Henry left for Saginaw at 6:00 p.m. with Brother Masons and after having supper, later discovered his friend Graff, waiting on the stair landing watching for him. They entered the lodge room and sat side by side and watched the degree work put on by the Detroit lodge, which all enjoyed immensely. Henry reached back home at 2:00 a.m.

Saturday, April 22, 1922

At 7:10 p.m., I was just coming home from near the church where I had been helping care for a sick friend, Charles Parkhurst, when I saw Graff drive by and on through town. When I reached home, he was visiting with Lucille. We all enjoyed a late lunch of apple pie, sandwiches, and cold tea, and then retired at 10:45 p.m.

Sunday, April 23, 1922

I slept soundly all night, never waking until 6:40 a.m. We had breakfast and a little later, Graff said, "Henry, let's walk down to the creek." They took their hats and left the room. Henry went out and fussed with the little chicks that had recently hatched. Graff, anxious to smoke, struck his match on the end of the woodshed, lit his cigar, and away they went.

Yes, Laddie, I know why you were restless today. Graff, do you recall when I asked you if you had any special new friendships? I wonder if you remember saying, "No, not anybody."

While the boys were outside, I fixed a box lunch of red raspberry pie, egg sandwiches, two kinds of cake, cookies, fried cakes, and toothpicks for the "bachelor boy" to take home with him. On their way back, they went across to the big barn with Vilas. Little Theo came running in and asked, "Grandma, where is Graff? I come to see him." I took her little hand in mine and went out to find him. When she saw him, she ran to him, and he took her in his arms and kissed her chubby cheek.

Henry was going to ride with Graff to see Mrs. Wildfong. So Graff took up his traveling bag and I said, "Here is a box you are to open after you get home."

He smiled and said, "I'll know how good it is when I sample it."

I wonder how he knew what was in it? He must have smelled the aroma of fried cakes hidden within. I carried the jar of dill pickles, and all was in readiness for his departure. He gave me my usual good-bye kiss, and we three stepped out to the car in front of the house. The boys entered the car, Graff said, "Good-bye, Ethel," and away they went round the corner and out of sight at 12:35 p.m.

Tuesday, May 23, 1922

Since I wrote last on these pages, one more of my dearest friends, Mrs. Susan Wildfong, has passed away. Henry had visited her just one month ago and came home to tell me of her illness. It seemed nothing could be done. Strange how we miss the touch of a vanished hand and the voice we loved so well. Though we will be separated for a time, we still have this assurance:

For I am persuaded, that neither death, nor life,
nor angels, nor principalities, nor powers,
nor things present, nor things to come,
Nor height, nor depth, nor any other creature,
shall be able to separate us from the love of God,
which is in Christ Jesus our Lord.

Sunday, May 28, 1922

Graff drove in from Vassar at 5:15 p.m. We visited for a while when Henry thought we ought to go call on Mother and Father Van. So he and I went to see them, and when we arrived, we discovered to our pleasure that Henry's brother Fred and wife Madge Van Wagnen from Jackson were visiting. We stayed and enjoyed a nice supper with them.

Thalia planned to take little Theo and go back with Fred and Madge in the morning for a two-week visit. Little Billy will be staying with me, so he came back home and was soon tucked into bed.

Monday, May 29, 1922

Today is Henry's fifty-second birthday. I was thankful that we had this family picture taken recently to present to him as a gift. It will be framed and placed in our home to cherish for years to come.

Front row: (left to right) Henry, John, and Ethel
Back row: (left to right) Lucille, Willard, and Thalia

Graff and I visited at the breakfast table in the kitchen. Time passed all too quickly as we recalled many happy incidents of the past years since we were girl and boy together.

He said, "Ethel, through all the long, long years, we've always been the truest and best of friends, and no home has ever been to me what your Old Homestead used to be in my boyhood and now your own home and Henry's. There is no place I love to go so well as to come here."

And reaching out and touching his hand, I said, "You must always remember, Graff, no matter where you are that I will always be the same dear friend that you have always enjoyed sharing your joys and sorrows with. It has been one of my joys to comfort and advise and help you when you have come to us from time to time. And if you have appreciated any kindness I have shown you, and it has helped to make your life brighter, I will not feel that I have lived in vain. And sometime, in the coming years perhaps it may be, I will be coming into your home as you have come into ours, and as we meet together from time to time, we must not let *new friendships* come between us and mar the pleasures that we all enjoy in each other's companionship. Our doors will *always* be open to you and yours, and you must feel that it will always be 'home' for you as long as you live."

Little Billy woke up and came out to us asking for "my dear Mama." I took him on my lap and told him that Mama and little Theo have gone way, way off to Jackson, and that he is going to stay and be Grandma's good boy.

Dear little man, his little lips quivered as he tried so hard to keep back the tears that gathered in his sweet brown eyes.

I know how hard it is, for often, I've felt as though I would give all I possess to be able to have a good cry when my heart was nearly breaking, and yet we have to learn to cover the bitter pain with smiles and words of cheer and comfort to those about us. And yet, how little the world or those around us realize that the one with the smiling face and cheery disposition is perhaps the *unhappiest* one of all.

About 10:30 a.m., we took Billy and walked down to the mill and saw Henry for a few minutes. Grandpa enjoyed the visit, but he could not hold and talk to Billy very long. Graff weighed himself on the scales and today only weighed 206 pounds. I had not gained an ounce since my illness in March, and I weighed just 133 pounds.

After our return to the house, Graff carried out his traveling bag and put it in the car and came in again and said, "Now, Ethel, if the weather is good and Henry gets his garden in shape and his *Tax Roll* done and off his hands, I will come down, and we can plan to leave for Londo Lake either the nineteenth or twentieth of June. That is less than three weeks from now. I will bring the smoked ham for you to boil and get ready for us to eat."

I wonder if our trip will prove as pleasant as it was the last. Let us hope that each cloud may have a silver lining and that we may have the same good, happy, and restful vacation we all so enjoyed last year. May we come home feeling it has done us all good to be together on another fishing trip.

Graff was all ready to leave for Midland and came in for his good-bye kiss. I told him to be careful. "Remember, the careful driver has to *look out* for the reckless one, and I always wonder what may happen before we see you again."

It was 11:20 a.m. and little Billy cried for Graff to take him, so he said, "Ethel, I'll take him for a ride around the block and then bring him back to you."

So they left me, and in a few minutes, Graff blew the horn, and I went out the front door to the car. We bid Graff good-bye and little Billy and were alone waving to him as he drove away from our sight.

Graff, this was the last visit I ever had with you as in the "days of our youth" when we shared our hopes and dreams with each other. As I looked back to the morning, you promised that you would never deceive me in any way, and you have faithfully kept your promise.

I shall never forget those words and what they meant to me.

Sunday, June 11, 1922

Since your last visit, Graff, my youngest boy Willard has gone out and away from me, leaving on the 2:00 p.m. train for Detroit. Little by little, as time goes by, my joys and comforts are slipping away one by one. And again, I had to stand by with the same old smile, knowing it was taking much out of my life, as the train slowly moved southward with him on board.

Saturday, June 24, 1922

Lucille secured a job setting type for the printing press at the Millington Gazette newspaper. About 9:00 a.m., she telephoned me from there and said, "Mama, there is a letter here for you."

So a few minutes later, I walked uptown for it knowing it was either from my boy Willard, or our dear friend Grafton.

Upon reaching the Gazette office, I found the letter with the Midland stamp on it. I opened it and found a few hurriedly written lines telling me Graff will be coming to Millington on Sunday, and *will bring his friend with him.* We will then fix the date for our fishing trip.

Sunday, June 25, 1922

The morning has dawned clear, bright and cool, one of many nice Sundays we've seen during the past fifteen months. For during the many, many Sundays Graff has spent with us, each day has been bright and pleasant.

Just now as I write these few lines, I'm wondering what the future Sundays will be like. I'm sitting by the west window waiting his arrival with his friend and thinking of the many pleasant hours we've spent with him in the past. I face the golden-lighted west and ask myself this question:

"What does the future hold for us? Our four, who have felt we lived for each other."

At 12:10 p.m., I was in the kitchen when Henry called to me, "Here they come!" And a moment later, I recognized Graff's voice and heard him introducing *Miss Gladys Dues* to Henry and Lucille. Then I passed through to the dining room and felt the warm handclasp and received my usual kiss from the big laddie. After which, he introduced his friend to me, and I felt at once that I will claim her for my friend.

Then I left them to visit, and I returned to the kitchen to finish preparing dinner. Soon all was in readiness as I put dinner on the table, and thus we enjoyed our first meal together.

After dinner, we went out to the shed to look over "The Trailer" that will convey most of our luggage and what nots to Londo Lake at the end of July. From there, we all went out to look at Henry's garden east of the barn. On our return, Graff said, "Now we must take some pictures." He went to the car for the Kodak and returned placing it in Lucille's hand.

She said, "Line up."

This is the first picture we had with Gladys, as Graff with an arm around each of us, kept us in line while Lucille did the rest.

Shortly after pictures were taken, Lucille and Gladys strolled along out into the backyard and Graff came over to me. Standing by the north window, he told me of his plans for the future and asked if I thought we could put off our fishing trip a little longer.

He lowered his voice and said, “Gladys and I will be married in one month on the twenty-fifth of July. If you can wait, we would all enjoy the trip together after that time and have Gladys make one of our number.”

I quickly replied, “Please don’t let us interfere with any plans you wish to make! Perhaps you would have a better time if you leave us behind, for you won’t care for extra ones along with you this time.”

But his eyes quickly filled with tears as he said, “Ethel, I want you all to go, and this must not *now* or *anytime* make any difference with our good times together. For you folks have made a home for me that is dearer than any other, and I shall want to come just as I’ve done before, and feel I can run in at any time and call it “home” as I have in the past.”

“And you know, nothing would please me more, Graff, than to have you *always remember and do that.* For I’ve been your friend so long and have learned that I too would miss your coming, for many times your presence has helped cheer me when my heart has been sad and heavy. And I will want Gladys to feel that she can come with you and enjoy the coming the same as you do. I will do all I can, Graff, to make her feel at home with us and will love her for her *own sake,* as well as yours.”

I hope we may often be together and as the months and years go by, we may all feel that five can have as good a time as four.

Shortly after our talk, the others returned to us, and Graff said, “We ought to take a ride. Where will we go?”

Henry replied, “Let’s go over to the hills. Gladys has never been there.”

So we all climbed into the Ford and left at 2:25 p.m. Our ride was a bit steep at times, but Graff drove with confidence so that none of us would have to get out and push. Shortly, we arrived at our destination, and Graff parked the car on the side of the road. We all exited and climbed up the hillside where we groped along through the bushes. Then after coming to a nice clearing, I called to them to stand still and "look this way." With Kodak in hand, I got this nice picture of them.

Upon our return to the car, we girls reported there was a flat tire. The boys quickly changed the tire and all was well again. Then on, we went to North Lake with the boys occupying the front seat. We stopped and went down to the lakeside for a walk and found a rude bench in a sheltered place.

We rested and visited for a short time. Then we returned to the car and left for the home trip by way of Otter Lake. We reached home at 4:50 p.m., and Henry immediately built the kitchen fire. I prepared lunch, which I nearly had ready when John, Maybelle, and their new baby arrived. After introductions, we celebrated our visit for the first time with the newest addition to our family—"Baby Norwood" by all enjoying supper together.

Maybelle and John

Soon after supper, Thalia and family came over and Graff held Theo and Billy on his lap.

Graff asked Thalia to favor us with a song, so she and Lucille went to the organ and sang:

"Let the Rest of the World Go By"

I listened as the girls lifted up their voices; Lucille seated on the stool at the organ, and Thalia stood beside her. The words of the song seemed to speak to my heart.

Is the struggle and strife we find in this life
Really worthwhile, after all
I've been wishing today I could just run away
Out where the west winds call.
With someone like you, a pal good and true
I'd like to leave it all behind and go out and find
Some place that's known to God alone
Just a spot to call our own.
We'll find perfect peace, where joys never cease
Out there, beneath a kindly sky
We'll build a sweet little nest, somewhere in the west
And let the rest of the world go by.

As they finished their song, the rest of us showed our pleasure with a nice round of applause. I'm not sure there weren't a few tears in some eyes. Graff seemed especially pleased and he asked for another. The girls agreed and sang:

"Leave Me With a Smile"

Their voices were raised again with a bit of a bounce to them and filled the old home with the melody and words:

Just like the sunrise you came to me it seems,
Just like the sunrise you woke me from my dreams.
You were my sunshine, in days that used to be;
I await the sunset, for now you're leaving me.
Tho' it's time for parting, and my tears are starting,
Leave me with a smile.
Tho' your heart may cry, dear;
When you say goodbye, dear,

Leave me with a smile.
Maybe it's forever, so while we're together,
For a little while;
Hold me like a flower, for one little hour,
And leave me with a smile.

We showed the girls our appreciation again with hearty applause, and then Thalia announced they must be heading home. We all said our good-byes to them as Lucille decided to write a song for Gladys.

After some time, Henry set off to do his chores, the girls went for a walk, and Graff and I visited. He said, "The girls are enjoying each other today."

Graff went into the kitchen, and I followed him with "these books," which he looked over and said, "Ethel, I'll always prize these books. I hope we will be able to have you write more of these trips, which we must have with Gladys in the future, for I'm sure she will want to come as bad as I will. I will be down before long again, and we will settle plans for our fishing trip and talk over the other plans for the future."

I shall look for your coming, Graff, for your "promise" is as sure as the rising and setting of the sun.

And now, as twilight settled around us once more, Lucille took this picture.

After this picture was taken, Graff turned to Gladys and said, "We must be going." I gave him his "book" to take back with him, and I carried out a vase of roses I had gathered from the backyard. I then handed a glass of milk to Gladys, and the big laddie drank two before he left the kitchen. Then we all made our way out to the Ford. We all realized that soon a new path would open before us, and it was with a feeling of sadness that I stood by and heard the farewell words spoken by the others and awaited my turn to say "good-bye."

Gladys had already stepped into the car and was waiting for a good-bye kiss. Then I turned to Graff, who took my hand and bent over, and pressed his lips to mine. He then stepped into the car, took his place at the wheel, and waved his hand in farewell. The car slowly rounded the same old corner at the north, and soon they were lost from our sight. Thus ended what seemed to be a happy day for the others in our party.

Sunday, July 23, 1922

We had received a good newsy letter from Graff last week saying he and Gladys were all through with the painting on the house and that it would be all settled by the end of the week. Then he will be down to make arrangements for our trip to the lakes next week. His time is getting short now, and we realize if he comes that only a few hours are left before we planned to go.

At 6:30 p.m., I was laying in the swing on the front porch when I heard the sound of an auto approaching and saw it was Graff and Gladys. The Sedan parked at the front of the house instead of in the south driveway. They departed the car and happily came up the walk and entered the Old Home. Henry and Lucille were already inside and before we could sit down, Graff started to speak.

We soon learned that Graff and Gladys had been married on Monday, July 17 at Standish! We all extended our "surprised" congratulations and managed to get a picture of the happy couple.

Their stay was a brief one, with only enough time to enjoy a light lunch. Afterwards, Henry took Graff to the garden and a little later, they came back with some raspberries to take home. Then the couple felt they needed to start for their new home at Bay City. They planned to return sometime Wednesday evening, so we will all be ready to leave for Londo Lake on Thursday, July 27.

We all went out to the car and good-byes were said. As Graff took his place and the car moved slowly away, I felt that the best friend I ever had was going out and away from us to enter a new life, which I pray may be a happy one.

He is the kindly friend
who often sits within my home
and chats with me awhile,
gives me the glory of his old-time smile,
and comes at times with willing hands.
No station high or rank this friend commands.
He too, must trudge as I,
the long days-mile, and yet
devoid of pomp or gaudy style,
he has a worth exceeding stocks or lands.
To him I often go, when sorrow's at my door.
On him I've leaned when burdens came my way,
Together oft we've talked our trials o'er,
And there is warmth in each "good-night" we say.

Graff, you are this friend, and now I am about to write the closing lines in this book, which I have rightly named *Golden Memories*.

And when I place it in your hands, it will be with this thought and wish that it will be the "golden link" in the chain of friendship that will never be broken.

In some way, Graff, I feel today as I try to see through the veil and look into the future that is stretching out before you, I have a presentiment that there will be times when you will want a friend. And then if that hour ever comes to you or yours, remember that back in the Old Home, if I am living, you will find me, just the same tried and true friend I've always been to you.

Chapter 15
Henry's Church

Looking Back to the 1880s

The Bailey Home—April 1892

"Ethel," called Mrs. Bailey, "Henry is coming up the road."

"I'm coming, Mama, I'm almost ready." Ethel was in her bedroom fussing, as she pulled her shoe on and grasped the button hook firmly in her hand. Then she began to work on the ten buttons that went all the way up past her ankle and had them done in no time. She quickly pulled on her other shoe and completed that as well. Ethel noticed that these old shoes were not looking like the latest styles she had seen in the catalogs lately, but for now, they would just have to do.

Henry Van Wagnen encouraged his horse to step it up as he neared the Bailey farm. Even though they had experienced a dry spell lately, the old dirt road was still full of deep ruts, and Henry didn't want to get his buggy stuck in one. "Get up!" he called out again and snapped the reins. His horse responded with a quick trot and snorted excitedly.

Henry was on his way to Ethel's home to have her attend church with him in Millington, and he certainly didn't want to be late. It was a bit overcast this morning, but no rain as yet. He hoped any chance of that would hold off until later in the day. Henry was anxious to escort Ethel today and after the service, take her to his home where his mother had planned somewhat of a feast.

Henry hadn't known Ethel growing up as they had attended different schools, but he had seen her in the past with her family in Vassar a few times. He was now twenty-two, and she was eighteen and had blossomed into quite an attractive young lady.

Henry had taken notice of Ethel one day when they both were in town shopping at the Vassar General Store and "ran into each other." Ethel had just come in from the cold, three-mile walk from her home. Her cheeks and nose were still stinging and her feet were just beginning to "thaw out." She had been lingering near the large potbelly stove during her shopping, hoping to soak in some warmth, when she saw Henry.

Ethel recognized him, but they had never been formally introduced. Henry stepped up to her and proceeded to present himself in such a friendly way. His hazel eyes seemed fixed on her as they spoke, and Ethel seemed to enjoy the young man's attention. They spent several minutes in pleasant conversation, which ended with Henry offering her a ride back to her home in his buggy. Ethel knew that she could at any time she was in town, visit and stay overnight with her girlhood friend, Charlotte Baker, and save her the long, cold walk back. But she gladly accepted Henry's kind invitation and was very flattered that he would take notice of her in such a way. She thought at first Henry was just being a gentleman, but it soon became apparent that he had more than a passing interest in her welfare. By the time they arrived at her home, he had asked Ethel if he could call on her in the near future, and she happily agreed.

After that, they attended various social functions together and thoroughly enjoyed each other's company. Ethel especially liked the dance at the Grange Hall and visits to the Vassar Opera House for lovely performances. They also enjoyed the church's young people's dinner and table games. There were, of course, many quiet meetings that the two shared. There were buggy rides through the countryside and visits at her home where they would take long private walks down wooded paths and around the farm.

Ethel finished pinning up a few locks of her long hair. She had fashioned them into a nice bun toward the top of her head. There were still some stubborn strands that were just not going to stay put, so she decided to leave them. They fell softly on the back of her neck and she reasoned that *no one would notice.* She smoothed the rest of her hair and checked herself in the mirror on her bureau dresser. She knew that the light blue dress she had selected was a favorite of Henry's. He wasn't shy about telling her that it was as pretty blue as her eyes. That made her believe that she was as dear to him as he was to her. Being with Henry made Ethel feel more grown up... *like a woman.*

Henry arrived at the Bailey home, and after greeting Mr. and Mrs. Bailey and engaging in some brief conversation with them, he helped Ethel pull on her heavy coat. Her mother insisted Ethel wear her wool bonnet and take the familiar bundle with her to the buggy. She had warmed a fieldstone on the stove and wrapped it in newspaper. It was about the size of a book, and Ethel knew to place it under her feet as they rode along for it would keep them warm for quite a while. Finally, everything was in readiness for their ride, and the young couple was on their way.

Ethel's family would be attending the little church a short distance from their home. It was actually the school where Ethel and the other Bailey children had attended, and on Sunday, a small number of people met there to worship. Visiting Henry's church was a new experience for Ethel, and she looked forward to it.

As they entered the buggy, Ethel placed the stone on the floor and sat down and covered her lap with the wool blanket that Henry had offered to her. These little comforts were much appreciated during the ten-mile ride since the weather was still quite cool. Henry and Ethel enjoyed pleasant conversation as they traveled and noticed the different scenes of interest and other travelers along the way. At last, the buggy pulled up to the Methodist-Episcopal Church in Millington.

The brick church with the stained-glass windows is the prettiest building in town, Ethel thought. Henry drove the buggy close to the church on the side street, where he quickly got out and tied his horse to the long hitching post. He helped Ethel down, and they walked briskly up the steps and into the church. As they entered the sanctuary, Ethel noticed two older ladies sitting at the front of the church glance her way and whisper to each other.

Henry removed his hat and when they were about halfway up the aisle, he motioned with his right hand to the pew. Ethel slipped into the shiny wood pew, and for a while, they sat alone. But not long after, another much older couple joined their row and sat nearest the aisle.

Soon, the organ began to sound out and indicated to the congregation the "Call to Worship." Reverend George W. Carter entered the front of the church through a side door and greeted the people. He was a young, stocky man with thick black hair and a smile that warmed the room. He seemed to Ethel such a friendly sort of fellow. He had a strong voice but not harsh as some other preachers she had heard.

After the Scripture reading, Rev. Carter said, "Please stand and turn to number 728 in your hymnals." Henry found the page quickly and offered to share with Ethel. The organist played a short introduction, and the congregation led by Rev. Carter began to sing.

What a friend we have in Jesus,
All our sins and grief to bear!
What a privilege to carry,
Everything to God in prayer!
Oh, what peace we often forfeit,
Oh what needless pain we bear.
All because we do not carry
Everything to God in prayer!

Ethel and Henry's voices seemed to blend in harmony. She, with her strong soprano, and he, with his perfect tenor, continued to sing the other verses. Ethel thought how well suited she and Henry were for each other, even their voices. When they had finished with "Amen," Ethel looked up at Henry and smiled. She was pleased to see he was smiling back and his eyes seemed to say, "Well done."

The service continued with some responsive readings, the Offering, and *The Lord's Prayer* followed by another hymn. Henry seemed to stand closer to Ethel as they again shared a hymnal and raised their voices with the congregation. By the last verse and chorus, Ethel was blessed by the beautiful words that rang throughout the sanctuary.

Jesus paid it all,
All to him I owe;
Sin had left a crimson stain,
He washed it white as snow.

The congregation was seated and settled in for Rev. Carter to begin his sermon. Henry seemed to be listening intently, but Ethel was having a hard time concentrating. Her thoughts seemed to wander from one thing to the next. She was excited to be invited to Henry's home for dinner today and was so looking forward to it. At times, she thought she could "feel" eyes watching her and quickly dismissed it as her imagination. If people were wondering what she was doing sitting next to Henry, they would just need to understand. After all, it was plain for anyone to see that she and Henry were a serious couple.

Ethel found herself fidgeting with her hands in her lap and then she would look at Rev. Carter and try to catch what he was saying. She glanced around the church at the various pictures on the walls, the dark mahogany furniture behind the pulpit, and the high ceiling. Everything was quite different from the plain little church she was used to attending. She found herself drawn to the beautiful colors in the stained-glass windows, and stared at them for some time. All in all, it was a sermon she hoped Henry wouldn't want to discuss with her later. She feared she had spent far too much time thinking about other matters, although she did remember a few points about "loving thy neighbor."

At last, Rev. Carter concluded his sermon with a short prayer for those among the congregation who were ill or unable to attend. Then he stepped down from the pulpit, stood looking out at "his flock," raised his right hand and pronounced the benediction:

The Lord bless thee, and keep thee:
The Lord make his face shine upon thee,
and be gracious unto thee:
The Lord lift up his countenance upon thee,
and give thee peace.
Amen.

At that, the chords from the organ came forth as Rev. Carter made his way down the aisle to the back of the church. He stood at the open doorway to greet everyone as they left.

Ethel gathered her coat and gloves off the pew as Henry turned to shake hands with Mr. Lane who had been seated behind him.

"Ethel," Henry began, "allow me to introduce Mr. and Mrs. Lane," he continued as he gazed back at her, "and this is Miss Ethel Baily." They all smiled and said hello.

Ethel noticed that Henry was very accustomed to the social graces and made everyone feel quite at ease. He had informed her that he had just recently become a member of the church, yet he seemed to be on friendly terms with everyone. He again helped Ethel with her coat, and they turned to enter the aisle as Mrs. Titsworth passed by her with a "Good day." She smiled and nodded the same reply. Then Henry and Ethel stepped out into the aisle and slowly walked toward the back of the church.

Rev. Carter was in position, smiling to each person, shaking hands, and having a few words with some. Ahead of them, Ethel heard Mrs. Titsworth tell Rev. Carter how much she enjoyed the sermon. She added that the singing seemed especially inspiring this morning as she glanced quickly behind her at Ethel.

Henry and Ethel stepped up to Rev. Carter, and they shook his hand and greeted him. He smiled and told them how happy he was to see them in the service. Ethel avoided commenting on his sermon, quite sure it would be a sin to pretend to have remembered much of it.

As they walked out to the steps, Henry donned his hat and offered Ethel his arm. She gladly took it, and they made their way to the buggy. Henry's horse waited, restlessly shifting his weight on his legs. After helping Ethel into her seat, Henry patted the horse's neck and untied the reins. He stepped up into the buggy and sat close to Ethel gathering the reins, and he gave them a little snap. Then with a click of his tongue, the horse jerked to attention and stepped out onto the little path that led from the churchyard.

Ethel gave a little sigh of relief and settled into her seat. She looked at Henry just as he turned to her and said with a shy grin, "My mother is fixing a special dinner for you today." She smiled back and took notice of how handsome Henry looked. He was a kind and gentle soul and had treated her with such a caring manner. He was a proper gentleman in public, not showing his affections outwardly toward her, but privately, he was attentive to her needs, and she felt he would provide well for her, if that day should ever come.

As the buggy made its way along, Ethel found herself thinking about a life with Henry. It had been a long time since she dared to entertain such thoughts. To do so had ended with much heartache and disappointment in the past. But perhaps now that she was older and quite ready for such a venture, the Good Lord might look kindly on her. She hoped that would be so.

It wasn't long before the buggy drove up to the house of the Van Wagnen family. Henry pulled up on the reins and stopped, jumped out of the buggy, and quickly tied it off at the post by the front gate. He turned to Ethel and held out his hand as she gathered her skirt and stood, taking his hand to steady her step down.

The Van Wagnen house was a nice-sized structure with white siding and a green roof. Mrs. Van Wagnen favored flowers around her home, and some purple crocus plants that lined the front path had already peeked out of the snow and were beginning to bloom. Forsythia bushes that grew on both sides of the house were fully green and waiting to burst forth their small yellow flowers. No doubt the yard would be filled with color by June.

Henry opened the gate for Ethel, and the two walked the short way to the front door. At once, the door swung open and Katie stood inside. "Come in!" she said with a grin, looking for all the world as if she was welcoming a long-lost relative. Henry's sister Katie was a year younger than Ethel, and he hoped that the girls would become good friends.

As soon as the couple stepped inside the house, there was a flurry of greetings and some introductions for those among the group who had not met Ethel. There were Henry's parents, Irvin and Anna Van Wagnen, along with brothers Martin (24), Olin (20), sisters Katie (17), Lora (16), Flossie (12), and the youngest, Fred who was six. Ethel took it all in stride, enjoying every moment of meeting Henry's family.

The aroma of fried chicken and biscuits filled the house, and Ethel's stomach grumbled. She was glad there was plenty of noisy chatter to keep anyone from hearing it. She offered to help in the kitchen, but Mrs. Van Wagnen declined, telling her, "Have a seat, dear. The girls will help if I need it."

So, she reluctantly found a high-backed chair near the fireplace. She was no doubt the center of attention in this setting, especially with the younger ones. After all, it wasn't every day that their brother brought a young lady home for dinner.

Lora kept busy by asking Ethel all sorts of questions, and Flossie busied herself by bringing some of her treasures and whatnots for Ethel to view. Fred sat quietly in a chair and amused himself by watching the girls fuss about.

After helping her mother in the kitchen, Katie came and stood by Ethel with a very serious look on her face and asked, "Do you know that we are having fried chicken for dinner?"

"Yes," replied Ethel in a happy tone, "and doesn't it smell delicious?"

"One of them is Henrietta," Katie said solemnly.

Ethel realized that Katie had apparently gotten attached to the chicken and named it. "I understand, because I did the same thing when I was a little girl," she teased as she hugged Katie, and both of them laughed.

In the meantime, Henry had taken a seat and was engaged in a lighthearted conversation with his father, Martin, and Olin about the local politicians and their latest ventures. Mr. Van Wagnen said that politics was always a good topic for causing indigestion.

The men chuckled at that remark, and then Henry's father began to recall some stories that had been handed down to him from his father. Ethel listened intently as he continued, saying he was told that "his people" came to this country from a town called Wageningen in the Netherlands. The family took upon themselves the name of the town, which became Van (from the town of) Wagenen.

Their ancestor was Aert Jacobson Van Wagenen, and he settled in the sheltered valley of Rondout in Ulster County, New York, about 1642. This was much like the land they had left so far behind.

Ethel noticed that the older man was quite clear about the details of his story, and she was eager to hear more. Mr. Van Wagnen stroked his gray beard and continued with tales of the hardships that were suffered from cruel winters, Indian attacks, and English soldiers demanding food and provisions. Through it all, the families kept their Dutch heritage and language for many generations. One way was to take the maiden name of the mother and give it to a son to carry on her name. Aert's wife was named Annetje Gerrits, and for many generations, the name Gerrit had been in their family. "It was my father's name, and his father's and great-grandfather before him."

Mr. Van Wagnen paused his story and looked at Henry and said in a proud voice, "Son, that is why your name is Garret Henry Van Wagnen." Henry seemed quite pleased with this part of the story, although it was not the first time he had heard it. Ethel smiled at Henry and felt so blessed to have been able to hear these stories and to be included in this special family tradition.

Just then, Katie came into the room and stood near her father, quietly waiting for him to finish. She leaned down toward him and said softly, “Dinner is ready, Father.” Mr. Van Wagnen nodded to her and slowly rose from his chair, which signaled to the rest of the family that at last it was time to come to the table.

And what a feast Mrs. Van Wagnen had prepared! Fried chicken was piled high on a large platter, and along with the biscuits, there was giblets and gravy, creamed corn, noodles, pickled beets, applesauce cake, and peach pies. There was so much talking and laughing that it made Ethel feel completely at home. She thoroughly enjoyed the company and Mrs. Van Wagnen’s delicious meal.

She even said a silent “toast” to Henrietta, who she had to admit, tasted better than her own pet chicken.

Chapter 16
Our Five

Millington, Michigan

Last year in June of 1921, "Our Four"—Grafton Gawne, Henry, Ethel, and Lucille Van Wagnen—went to Londo Lake on an eight-day fishing trip. We all enjoyed it so much, we decided that if all were alive and well, we would go again in 1922.

July 26, 1922

On Wednesday evening, our dear friend Grafton Gawne and bride Gladys of 400 S. Hampton Street, Bay City, drove in to be here on time for an early start tomorrow for Londo Lake.

Thursday, July 27, 1922

All up in good season, had our breakfast, and the boys hustled to get our belongings loaded. Our son John drove up and left the horse team out in front of the house. Lucille got a picture of the new little bride standing beside the horses while John came in to say good-bye.

Our kind friend Abner String had loaned us his trailer, and soon all our necessary belongings were packed, and we were ready to go. Lucille now refers to the trailer as "Abner."

At 8:30 a.m., we asked our neighbor Wilma to come over and take our picture just as "Our Five" are ready to step into the Ford. We all looked pretty good-natured, and the girls seem to feel proud of their clean, white shoes and stockings. *Don't you think we looked quite nice?*

Left to right: Graff, Ethel, Henry, Gladys, and Lucille

Then we bade Wilma good-bye, stepped into the car, and away we went. After a few miles, Henry asked, "Which way are we going?" No one in the backseat seemed to know whether we were going north, south, east, or west. Ha ha. But, twas enough to know we were on our way and hoping for a happy day.

A pretty little butterfly came in the window, and I carefully caught it and put it back outside. It may bring us good luck. We passed the barnyard where we turned around last year when the road was all torn up. Today, the road was all nicely paved.

Soon Gladys announced, "Here is Bay City. Look at the new high school building, which cost $3,000,000!" *Mercy that's a lot of money!*

At 10:09 a.m., we arrived at Graff and Gladys' home where he parked the car near the driveway, and we all got out. He hurriedly unlocked the door, and we entered their new home for the first time. We looked over their rooms and saw how nice and cozy they are going to be. Gladys started dinner and Lucille helped her, while the boys were out putting the extra luggage on the trailer.

Gladys asked me to find and pack what articles of wearing apparel, etc., that I knew Graff needed to take with him. I did not forget to put in his razor and strap, for I knew he would want to shave, and then Henry might want to try to use it this year and see if it would cut any better than it did last year.

We had things nearly in readiness when Gladys wanted to set the dining room table. But I said, "No, we'll eat in the kitchen and save time." So we sat down and enjoyed our first meal with them. Everything tasted good. I got the boiled ham on the big stew kettle and put on a tight cover. Graff rushed out and put two big cabbages into the car. He went back to the house and carried out some heavy curtains to take along. *Did you ask what are they for?* Oh, maybe to cover up if it gets too cold. We reentered the car at 12:30 p.m., and Graff called, "All ready?" We said *go!*

Not long, we stopped at the store where Graff bought a rope and Henry got some new overalls. A few minutes later, we crossed the river bridge, and Lucille found she had broken the mirror in her purse. Too bad. *Hope it doesn't bring us any bad luck.*

We arrived in Standish and stopped at the Courthouse at 2:10 p.m. Graff went in to look for the bill folder that had been misplaced. He thought he may have been excited on Monday, July 17 when he and Gladys were married and left it there. He soon returned without it. Tis a pity, for he had a few pictures in it that I wanted for his book. But if he doesn't find the folder, we will have to take some more pictures to put in their place.

We hadn't traveled too far when Graff said, "Blow out!" We all got out and found the tire *flat.* We girls crossed the ditch and sat down beside the fence, while the boys got busy and removed the tire.

I called, "Graff, look here." He turned our way and just at that instant, Lucille caught him, never thinking it would be the last one with that same old smile for some time.

Soon all was ready again with another tire on. The boys wiped sweat from their faces and called "Come on." And we girls were only too glad to step into the car and get out of the hot sun.

Down the road, Graff tried to see how near he could come to hitting the rear end of a load of hay as he came up the hill. We enjoyed a ride of six minutes' duration when the big lad called, "Another flat tire!" Ha ha. We all got out again and sat beside another fence. Graff discovered he had left his tire glue at home, and we had the laugh on him. But, never mind, someone will come along soon and you can buy, borrow, or steal some, *maybe.* But you had better buy or borrow. Graff halted the third car before he got anyone who had glue. Both cars stopped, the man in the second car proved to be George Hall of Caro, a former supervisor whom Henry knew when both were supervisors a few years ago. Henry introduced me, and I visited with the ladies in the car. Soon Graff had the tire fixed and at 4:00 p.m., we were on our way again.

We arrived in Prescott on M-70 when Graff stopped at a garage to purchase some glue. The afternoon was already getting pretty warm when I asked Henry to step in and ask if they were giving away fans that were in the window. The lady said, "No, they are for sale. How many ladies have you in your car?"

Henry told her, "Three."

"Well, I'll give them each one as a souvenir of Standish."

He thanked her and brought them to the car to us. We girls each took one and immediately put them to good use. Then Graff came back to the car, and I gave him a drink of cold tea. After he finished it, we were on our way again.

We saw a big hill ahead of us, and I told Graff he had better stop and let us all get out and walk up as we had a heavy load. But he said, "No, sit still, I'll make it." He *gave her the gas*, but just before we reached the top, we felt the car slow to a stop and then began to roll backwards. Henry attempted to get out, and Lucille tried to go at the same time. The car door was too narrow, and they clogged the way and neither of them got through.

Henry raised his voice excitedly and said, "Holy Moses, can't you let a man get out?"

Lucille finally got squeezed back into the seat, and her father jumped out and blocked the wheels. Then we all got out and did our part and pushed. After a few minutes, we reached the top with the women laughing enough to split our sides.

Henry frowned, "I don't see anything funny to laugh about. We might have all been tipped over and hurt."

I got control of myself and answered, "Yes, but we weren't, and even if we had, I would have been laughing anyway to see you and Lucille *crowd so.* No one would ever think you had any manners to see you push each other!"

At 5:15 p.m., Graff called out, "See the lake!" And sure enough, we caught glimpses of its clear smooth water.

Very soon, we hit the lakeside driveway and I said, "Graff, look out for that sink hole. Let us get out." But once more, he is confident that he can get through. Alas, he found he would have to let us get out and help again.

Do you remember me telling you just before we left home that the girls were proud of their white shoes? Well, they have nothing to be proud of now, for they are all muddy, and our feet are wet after helping get the car out. But we all kept cheerful and soon rounded the same old corner and past where our tent I had called Look Out Cottage stood last year. We went up the hill and opposite the farmhouse on the hill where we halted and exited the car.

Henry cut stakes, and the boys pitched our tent, which I promptly named "See All Cottage."

At 5:45 p.m., a big car drove up and stopped beside us, and we discovered twas our friends from Millington—Albert and Lillie Cobb and their two children. We hailed them with delight, and they too were glad to have us as their neighbors. They decided to pitch their tent just across the way from us.

We all got busy: set up cots, unloaded the trailer and car, unpacked, hung up clothes, and then Lucille and I began to prepare our supper. And oh, how we did enjoy our first meal! We were all very hungry after the long day, and everything tasted good.

I withstood the trip very well, considering how badly I was feeling. Much of it was due to my having confidence in the careful driver at the wheel, so I did not get very tired or nervous.

The boys rented boats at once to be sure to have them in the morning. That night, we all retired quite early and rested pretty well considering our outdoor sleeping arrangements.

Friday, July 28, 1922

We were all up and feeling fine at 5:30 a.m. and out on the lake to try our luck. Graff moved slowly away from the shore in the boat with Gladys and Lucille. Gladys got the first catch and Lucille got two pike; enough to clean for breakfast. Henry and I rowed around for some time but got hardly a nibble, and we finally went back. We found that Gladys and Lucille had breakfast about ready, and we all enjoyed our first catch of fish.

A little later while we were all outside our tent, Gladys and I were sitting on the trailer watching the others when Lucille said, "Sit still and I'll take your picture." *We never moved.*

I had not been well for many weeks, and it seemed at first as though I would never endure this trip. But as day after day went by and the time drew nigh, I felt I must not give up for the sake of the others. So, I tried to forget myself in the thought of making the others happy. And it did not require any effort on my part to sit still for this picture.

At 10:30 a.m., Graff called, "Let's take a ride." So, we all stepped into the car and away we went on a new road for us. After crossing through some fields, we came upon a bridge at Dace Lake. Graff pulled up and parked the car and immediately Henry exclaimed, "See that horse way out in the lake!"

And sure enough, far out in the lake, we saw two horses wading in the water two thirds up their back. They soon left the lake and calmly came up to land near us. We ladies got out and carefully went to pet them. They were beautiful, dark brown mares, and both stood quietly as we patted their necks and talked to them. As we fussed over the horses, Graff and Henry looked around the area for a possible campsite.

Graff said, "I don't think we will better ourselves by moving here Henry. We will stay where we are at Londo Lake even if it doesn't have any *sea horses*." Henry chuckled and agreed.

We arrived safely back at See All Cottage at 12:50 p.m. The boys soon had a good campfire going, and we girls got busy at once preparing dinner. We had new potatoes from our home garden, Graff's boiled ham, bread, butter, honey, mince pie, and tea. Then we all sat down around "our table," which Graff and I had fitted up so nicely to accommodate five. Graff sat at one end, Gladys next to him on his left, and Lucille beside her. Henry and I sat on my "Black Box" while the others all had camp chairs.

After dinner, Graff went across the road to the big barn where some men were working. While there, he offered to build their grain stack for the owner, Mr. McGoon.

Gladys and Lucille took their books and went down toward the lake, stopping beneath the shade of some trees where they sat down to read.

Henry and I got in a boat and rowed out on the lake. I called to Lucille that she will have to cook all the fish I bring back. She replied, "All right, bring up a good big mess."

We were gone for some time and returned without any. I saw the girls were having fun by the trees, so I went and got in the car to rest. I was pretty tired and lame, so I found a comfortable spot and began to read my book.

Graff soon came along from across the road, stopped beside the car, and told of his success in building the grain stack. Then he said, "The girls are having their pictures taken." He looked at me and was dead serious. "I won't ever have another picture."

Surprised at his words, I said, "Graff, you must not be jealous." He gave me one passing glance and stepped through the fence, passing into the shaded woodland beyond and was lost to my sight.

You will not wonder he thought he was left out when you see how many pictures the girls had without him. Ha ha.

Girlfriends

Gladys on fence

After a short time, Graff returned and entered the tent and lay down on their cot. The girls came up, and Lucille went across the road and sat in the shade to write a letter. Gladys went into the tent, but soon came back out over to me. She and I visited a few minutes, and then I went to help Lucille find the new pencil she had lost in the grass under the tree. I quickly found it, and she was happy again.

Lucille in tree

Gladys and I visited once more. She seemed a bit dejected, so I told her I was going into the tent to talk to Graff. All was quiet within, and I found him laying down, with hands folded on his chest unmindful of the book he had laid open beside him. Bending over him, I said, "Hush, Laddie. There is something I want to say to you."

For several moments, I talked to him about our trip, how we were looking forward to such a happy time, and that he must not creep away and leave us. For if he did, it would take all the joy away from the rest of us; *for he was the life of our party.* We could not let anyone sleep or be away from the rest of us for very long.

Graff listened quietly, and I finally left him alone and went out of the tent. *I told Gladys to go in and keep him company.* Poor fellow, he didn't realize what he had on his hands when he started out to take his vacation and get a little rest. With three women to torment him and keep him from reading or sleeping, *what one of us could not think of the other would.*

Lillie Cobb came over from her tent with some pictures and a post-card of the Soo Locks to show Henry.

While they were visiting, I went back to the tent to see if Gladys was successful in keeping Graff from going to sleep. I found her beside him with one arm around his neck and her face down close to his. I asked if I was intruding and both said, "No, come on in." So I sat down beside them.

I was *deeply touched*, and laying a hand on each of them, I said, "*You remind me of two children in one way*, in another tis more than child's play, when you think of the future. Today, you have been married thirteen days and when we think of the future and what it holds for you, *much depends on how kind and loving* you can be to each other".

"Life is short at best, if you love each other dearly and make the best of every day and hour. Sometimes even when we think we have chosen wisely and well, we meet with many disappointments along life's journey. I have been your best friend, Graff, since your early boyhood, and there is *no one* who wishes you a *happier life* than I do. I know how much you can do to make a happy life for Gladys, but in making each other happy, you will have to learn that there will be times when *you can't always have your own way*. Then again, it will be her that will have to be the one to bring peace and joy to you."

I looked fondly at them and continued, "What I've been to you, Graff, I want to now be to Gladys too. So, if I can help either of you, always remember that you have only to ask for me to come at any time. For as the months and years go by, I shall not forget you, and shall hope and pray that your lives may be happy ones. I'm sure Gladys will do her part. *Graff, will you give me your promise that you will do yours?*"

With eyes dimmed with tears, he looked into my face and gave me his promise. I bent over him and pressed my lips to his. Then I leaned toward Gladys and left a long lingering kiss on her cheek. *God bless you dear ones.* Then I silently walked out of the tent and returned to the car where I sat alone.

Graff and Gladys spent the rest of the afternoon communing in the tent. They could be heard visiting and laughing until nearly five o'clock. At that time, we all decided to go out trolling and see what luck we would have today. We found our luck was poor as ever and came in empty-handed. So we had our supper and all retired early.

Saturday, July 29, 1922

We are all up at 5:40 a.m. I did not get any sleep last night, so I did not feel like getting up so early; but "*If you are in Rome, do as the Romans do,*" so I climbed out.

Graff and his bride went out fishing, while Henry, Lucille, and I set out in the other boat. We did not get many strikes, but I finally landed a good, big pike. Shortly after, Lucille got a small one. Then we decided to come back to camp and have some breakfast.

Gladys hanging from a tree

Lucille perched on a gate

After breakfast, we all fussed around the tent and fire until the afternoon when Graff and Gladys once more made sail for the boat. They did very well and came back with twenty-two blue gills.

At 5:10 p.m., Graff decided we would drive to Hale for a few supplies. We reached there and the girls went to the post office to write and mail cards while Henry hustled over to the barbershop. He found too many ahead of him and decided he wouldn't wait for a shave but would be "grizzly" over Sunday. Instead, Henry went to the store and bought two loaves of fresh bread, one pound of creamery butter, cards, and post stamps.

After Henry returned to the car, we sat and visited while Graff went for his purchases, which included tobacco, arsenic of lead, and bread for Mrs. McGoon. The girls returned bringing ice cream cones for all. We ate ours, and Gladys gave me one to keep for Graff. Twas a wonder I kept it until he returned from the store. *Someone was going to have to lick it before it melted!*

We all climbed back in the Ford and started back to See All Cottage reaching there at 6:40 p.m. At that time, Graff, Gladys, and I decided to go out trolling. We girls got two nice pike apiece and then headed back to the tent. Upon reaching there, we found Henry and Lucille had a nice warm supper waiting for us with fried potatoes, fried fish, bread and butter, fried cakes, and tea. My, but it tasted good.

Then Graff and Gladys thought they would go out and clean our fish. Graff tried to get up from the table, but the space between the table and tent post *seemed a lot narrower than when he sat down* to eat, and he nearly ruined his camp chair.

Later in the evening, Lucille and Graff built the bonfire, and he fixed one in the pan to smoke the mosquitoes out of the tent. The girls were happy and sang songs long after the rest of us retired.

Sunday, July 30, 1922

Henry and Graff were the first ones up, then one by one, we girls sprung off our cots and dressed. Lucille took the lead and fried the fish. I made coffee, and after a busy half hour, we finally heard the breakfast bell ring. After eating, we all busied ourselves: Henry went to visit Albert, the girls walked down to the lakeside, and after I had made up the cots, Graff decided to lay down for a nap. I then cleared the table, made some sandwiches, and fixed some other items to put in my lunch basket. Graff had mentioned that we would go for a drive later and eat our dinner in the quiet hills somewhere. Thus we all spent a restful Sunday morning.

Later, when all arrived back at camp, our plans changed when all agreed to *stay put* and enjoy our "picnic" meal right there. As we were visiting around the tent, Mr. and Mrs. Bert Noonan of 615 Queen St., Owosso, Michigan, drove up. He had been to Hale with her to see the doctor. The evening before, she fell off the barnyard gate and nearly broke her ankle. I went to the car to find the necessary items and returned to Mrs. Noonan. I applied liniment, gave it a good rubbing, and fixed a bandage for her.

She sighed in relief and said, "Thank-you, dear lady. That certainly makes it feel better." I offered to dress it morning and night while we stayed there and she gladly accepted my offer.

At that time, a car passed by us, and almost immediately, we looked down the road and discovered it had gone in the ditch. We all went down to see if either men were hurt. Thankfully, they were all right, so Lucille quickly took this picture of the wreck. *By the looks of that missing wheel, I don't think they are going anyplace soon.*

The remainder of the "Sabbath" afternoon was spent resting, quietly strolling the lakeshore, and visiting with our camping neighbors Albert and Lillie.

At 4:00 p.m., in the far distance, I heard the faint roll of thunder and saw the flash of lightning. I went out to the car and got in the rear seat and sat there alone to watch the approaching storm. But, somehow, I did not feel afraid or anxious in any way. I suppose my mind was in sympathy with the elements, for they did not disturb me. I sat there during the long, hard downpour and noticed that the others hustled to the tent for cover.

After the storm had somewhat abated, I left the car and went to the tent and asked Henry to build a fire so I could fix supper. He thought I was *crazy* and told me so. *He did not realize how near he spoke the truth.* Ha ha.

"I don't know what you think you can cook out here in this rain that will be fit for us to eat!" he said in disbelief.

"Never mind," I replied, "just get busy and build the fire." He did so, then I ordered him to go with the others and keep out of the way.

In a short time, I gave the call that supper was served, and all responded by getting into their respective places at the table. When I began serving them, Graff said, "Vegetable soup, that's the best of everything yet. What other surprises do you have in that black box?" Henry had to admit that he enjoyed my "surprise" too.

After our hearty meal, I left the girls to clean up, and I went down to care for Mrs. Noonan's ankle. We had a nice visit and then I made my way back to See All Cottage. At 9:30 p.m., we all decided it was time for some sleep and we soon retired.

Monday, July 31, 1922

Graff called to us from outside the tent, "Get up, folks. Tis a good morning for trolling. Let's get out on the lake." Henry heard a few scattering raindrops on our tent and hesitated. But he finally did get up, and the rest of us followed. Graff took the girls with him, and they all headed to the lake in hopes of a big catch.

Henry and I pushed off just a few minutes after the others, but they were nowhere in sight. As our boat slipped onto the water, a heavy mist that lay on the lake like a cloud surrounded us. It seemed to be a glimpse of heaven as we quietly moved across the water, which was as smooth as glass. It was such a beautiful and peaceful setting that I didn't mind that the fish were not biting. Let them be. I was content to drift along and enjoy the scene that would soon be melting from our sight.

I slipped my hand over the edge of the boat and let my fingers touch the surface of the water as we floated along. Henry sensed that I was enjoying the ride, so he continued rowing, not bothering to fish either. The only sounds that entered our solitude were the old wooden oars as they dipped quietly in the water and the mournful wails of the lake loons calling to each other. Their sound carried across the lake as one waited on the other to answer. Once, I caught sight of the bird silently gliding along the misty water before it dove and then disappeared from sight. I told myself to capture those moments of tranquility in my mind so that someday I could recall the peaceful days at Londo Lake. For, who knows if we shall pass this way again?

Whereas ye know not what shall be on the morrow. For what is your life? It is even a vapour, that appeareth for a little time, and then vanisheth away.

Henry and I enjoyed our voyage, and after a time, my dear husband turned the boat and headed back to shore. When we arrived at See All Cottage, the others were already there to tell us they too had no luck. Graff said he thought that the pike were lying too low this morning.

Lucille started breakfast, and I went across the road to see how Mrs. Noonan's ankle was. I found that she and Bert had slept on the haymow in the barn last night on account of the storm. We helped her to a soft seat on some hay, and I bathed and bandaged her ankle. Then we set her on the two-wheeled cart, all ready for her bumpy ride down the hillside to their camp, which I had named "Mosquito Point."

I returned to headquarters and reported that I was ready for breakfast. Lucille served us fried fish, bread and butter, fried cakes, and coffee. Later, I told Gladys she had better get Graff's cabbages on to cook with that piece of ham or else Henry would have the raw cabbage all eaten up. She agreed and quickly put the ham and cabbage in a big pot on the fire to cook.

Then Gladys came to me and said, "Graff and I are going over to South Londo. Come with us, won't you?" As I was not feeling well, I thought I would be poor company. So, I begged to be excused and left them to enjoy their trip alone. I then got into the car to crochet and keep watch of the fire. When they returned, I had dinner all ready.

We all enjoyed the one-pot boiled dinner of ham, cabbage, carrots, potatoes, and onions. Henry liked the "juice" drippings over his potatoes. I noticed that we had eaten the last of the mince pie yesterday, and I had only one fried cake left. I asked the boys if they wanted it cut into five pieces for dinner. They both said, "Yes!" Ha ha. We each got one little bite.

Graff asked me, "Do you have anything more to make delicious soup like we had last night?" *Sorry, Laddie, nothing left.*

We put in the afternoon doing odd jobs and visiting until 3:00 p.m. Then Lucille got her father started and with Gladys, they went out "still" fishing. They left Graff in the tent on his cot trying to sleep among the flies and mosquitoes. I was busy in the car working on crocheting my dresser scarf.

Later, I discovered the pan of apple sauce that Lillie had cooked for us was sitting in the trailer bed where Lucille had left it. Rather than see the flies carry it away pan and all, I laid my work down and took it inside the tent. I found Graff wide-awake sitting on the edge of his cot, so I stayed there a while and visited with him.

When the *fisherfolks* returned, they said they didn't get a bite. We decided to go for a visit to our "jolly neighbors" Albert and Lillie. Lucille took along her Kodak and said, "Let's have a picture."

Lillie had just come from the pump with a two-quart can of fresh water and she was thirsty, too. Henry was hungry, and Albert was trying to feed him something with a big spoon, and Henry's mouth looked like a young robin's. I felt as though I was slighted and could only look on, as they didn't offer me even a good drink of water. My, we were a comical looking bunch!

Left to right: Lillie, Cleo, Albert and Ilene Cobb, Henry and Ethel

Tuesday, August 1, 1922

Graff was the first one up and went out in such a rush that I thought sure from the racket I heard that he had tipped the trailer and its contents over. But upon investigation and inquiring later, I learned he had just run into a bunch of pigs. He had hit one with such force that he knocked it clear through the big tank that was lying beside the fence. Oh dear, I just laughed until my side ached, but Graff didn't think it was any laughing matter. *Can you smile now, Laddie?* I finally got sobered down, and we got a nice big breakfast ready. By that time, we were all ready to eat. *Bacon anyone?*

Then plans were made to go to Hale, so we hustled around with "our housework." I went out to see if the boys were ready and discovered Graff *on his knees* beside the car. But upon moving up quietly so as not to disturb him, I found he was only fixing a tire. Poor fellow, he was having a hard time, but you know, the darkest hours are just before the dawn, so when the patch was on and all in readiness, he felt better.

Just before we got started, Mr. and Mrs. Noonan came over to have me bathe and bandage her ankle. Mr. Noonan said he would like a picture with me fixing up her ankle and I said, "If you're not afraid of spoiling your Kodak."

Mrs. Noonan and I posed with swollen ankle, liniment bottle, old felt shoe, crutches, and last but not least, Mrs. Noonan in Bert's baseball suit. Even my curtains in the car window look good. *Don't you think we look natural?*

I returned to camp and Graff said, "Now, Ethel, if you are ready, we will get started for Hale." I had abandoned my khaki suit and put on a clean gingham dress, but the girls didn't want to change theirs. So when the others were ready, I called to the girls, and they said they wouldn't go, so I told Graff, "The girls in khaki are not going with us."

He answered, "All right, let them stay home." He then called to Henry, and they stepped quickly into the car and took the front seats. I sat in the rear seat and away we went at 11:00 a.m. After we reached Hale, Henry went at once to the barbershop for he needed a shave very badly. Graff kept me company in the car.

He was very quiet and thoughtful on this day. It seemed a very big undertaking was on his mind and for old friendship's sake, I tried to advise and help him by giving him helpful hints and begged him not to be hasty in his judgment and decision or all would be lost.

"Take time to consider and have patience, Laddie boy, and in God's own good time, you will not be sorry you listened to me. We all meet with obstacles and disappointments and stumble along, and then after many, many years, we learn the things that for so long we have yearned to know."

Graff, you have had years of experience and I have often thought of your kindly offer of assistance to me many years ago when you said, "Ethel, if the time ever comes when you need a friend and I can help you in any way, you have only to ask or send and I will come."

Today, Graff, it is my good fortune to be with you when you need help and so I plead with you not to be hasty, and although you have promised this man, "the blacksmith," that you will go back to Hale after you take us back to the tent.

"Don't go back Graff, please don't!"

Do you know why? I leave the answer with you.

Well, Henry came back to the car clean shaven and brought me a letter from Thalia. He got in the car with me while I read the letter from home and found all was okay there. Graff went after some fresh bread for Mrs. McGoon, and then away we went for Londo Lake.

Upon our arrival at See All Cottage, I had a long visit with Gladys about housekeeping and making her home life a happy one by being kind and loving to the big lad who had taken her into his care and keeping.

Gladys, I've known him for years and have helped him over some rough places and you will do well to remember that kind words will soothe and calm his ruffled spirit more quickly than angry words. Just think of this old saying:

"Angry words! O let them never, From the tongue unbridled slip,"

With Lucille's help, we finally got dinner on and sat down to eat. Henry and Lucille finished first and excused themselves and went outside. Graff, Gladys, and I sat at the table and visited. Finally, I asked Graff, "What time will you be ready for supper?"

He said, "Anytime you say."

"All right. Supper at 5:00 p.m. Then will we all go trolling?"

He hesitated for a second and then replied, "Yes, Ethel, I'll be here."

I knew at once that I had won, and he would not be returning to Hale to see the blacksmith. Reaching out and laying my hand on his, I said, "Thank you."

Graff, you are a good old scout.

Chapter 17
Permission

Looking Back to the 1880s

Ethel sat quietly on her bed, while she fondly touched the soft, green velvet cover of the Autograph book on her lap. It had been given to her last night, and such a pleasant surprise it was. She turned to the first page and reread the note that was carefully written:

Presented to Ethel E. Bailey
By Henry Van Wagnen
May 9, 1892

She thought how shy Henry had acted when he gave it to her as they sat in his buggy. She had expected Henry to mention his intentions toward her, but all he said was, "I'll be speaking to your father tomorrow."

Ethel's heart beat with excitement, but she managed to smile and say, "That will be fine." A proposal of marriage didn't really need to be expressed between them. After many months of courting, everyone including Ethel expected it.

Henry, true to his word, arrived at the Bailey farm bright and early the next morning. After stepping into the kitchen and greeting the family, he asked Mr. Bailey if he could speak to him outside. Ethel, who was standing by her mother at the stove, glanced at Henry when he turned to walk out and saw the calm look on his face. She was not so calm as she watched Papa rise from the kitchen table and follow Henry out the door. Her mother sensed the importance of the moment and reached up to her daughter and put her hand on Ethel's cheek. "He's a good man, dear. I'm sure your papa will approve."

Henry slowly walked from the porch toward the maple trees a little way from the house. He didn't want anyone in the house to hear, but he also didn't want Mr. Bailey to have to walk very far. The maples seemed just about the right distance. Mr. Bailey didn't speak as they made their way, and Henry rehearsed in his mind again what he would say.

When they reached the spot, Mr. Bailey looked up at the trees and remarked how big they were getting. Henry nodded in agreement and Mr. Bailey proceeded to sit down in a nice cool, grassy spot next to a large tree. Out of respect for the older man, Henry joined him sitting down on the grass. The men started talking about the crops and the recent warm weather. Henry was beginning to get nervous and was half listening as he thought of a way to change the subject. Mr. Bailey reached for a tall blade of grass and pulled it up revealing a tender green tip, which he promptly put in his mouth and began to chew. As he stroked his beard and stared at the tilled fields stretching out in front of him, Mr. Bailey asked, "What's on your mind, son?"

Henry took a deep breath and asked for Ethel's hand in marriage. The words spilled out so quickly, Mr. Bailey turned and stared at Henry's serious face for a moment and then chuckled softly. He agreed to the marriage, and before he could say another word, Henry was telling him of his intentions to work hard and support Ethel, find a home, and various other plans that a young man would want for his new wife. Mr. Bailey didn't have any words of advice as he slowly stood up, stretched, and started back toward the house. "I best be gettin' to work."

Henry stood under the maple trees as he watched Mr. Bailey walk back to the house. He was walking with a slight limp, something Henry had never noticed before. All he could think about was how happy he was and the look on Ethel's face when she found out what her father said.

By the time Henry got back to the house, the news of the proposal had thrilled the entire household. Henry entered the house and stood just inside the doorway. He looked at Mrs. Bailey, who seemed to be smiling and crying at the same time. Ethel, so happy with the news her father shared, ran across the kitchen to him and hugged his neck. They both laughed while Mr. Bailey stepped back, looked at his grown daughter, and tried not to think about her leaving. She was, of course, his "dear Ethel."

Henry felt a bit out of place with the family's display of emotion. But after some hugs and handshakes with the others, he persuaded Ethel to come with him to take a short walk and bring the Autograph book with her. She happily consented, and the newly engaged couple walked hand in hand out behind the barn.

Later that night, Ethel again sat on her bed looking at the little book. Henry had wanted to be the first one to write in it. In the years to come, she would have others sign it. Some would write a humorous saying, a friendly poem, or just sign their name. Henry took this occasion to seal his intentions toward her, and he hoped that she understood the love that was behind it.

Friend Ethel:
May our friendship be not
Like flowers that fade,
But the evergreens that
Flourish forever.

Your true friend,
Henry Van Wagnen

Ethel thought about her new life with Henry. They planned to be married in September, just four short months away. Her life here on the farm with her family would soon be over, and the thought of leaving them made her cry a little. There would be no more carefree childhood days spent here.

Thoughts of Graff came into her mind, and she felt sorry for him and a little guilty about her own happiness and plans. He was still helping run the farm, and his brothers and sisters depended on him so much.

She hoped someday he would continue his life and find a bright future and the happiness he so deserved.

Ethel closed the book and held it to her heart. She whispered a prayer, thanking the Good Lord for all her loved ones and earnestly asked that His will be done.

Chapter 18
Our Future

Londo Lake Fishing Trip
The afternoon of August 1, 1922

Our Five continue to enjoy our time together.

After our tasty lunch, I left the tent and entered the car. I tried to read my book but felt that I could neither read nor crochet. The intense strain of the past few days has kept my head hurting so badly that at times my eyesight almost left me. Just at this time, the pain in my head was so severe that I found a small blood vessel had burst and my eye was all black where the blood had settled around it.

Doctors have told me that these headaches and my heart spells are due to my sickness with rheumatic fever as a girl so long ago. I did not know at the time what harm it had done, or what the future would hold for me. Oh well, such is life.

After a while, Gladys came out of the tent with a happy smile on her face and walked over to me. *I'm glad "Girlie" to see that pleasant look on your face, for I know you and Graff have enjoyed the afternoon being together.* I did my best to keep the others away from the tent and let you enjoy yourselves visiting alone.

The girls thought they would enjoy a plunge in old Londo waters. Gladys looked pretty frail, but if we could stay long enough, we would fill her up on fish.

Gladys

I've never fixed up any special food for Lucille, for she seems to thrive on anything I feed her. "Poor girl."

Lucille

Never mind Gladys, Graff is a good provider and if you prove to be a good cook, in time you may outweigh her yet.

I had supper ready at 5:00 p.m. sharp. The big lad had been true to his promise and did not go back to Hale to see the blacksmith. Instead, he stayed close to the tent all afternoon. "Good boy!"

After supper, Graff took his bride, and they went out trolling. The rest of us went out too, but no one was successful with the fish so we soon returned to the tent. We spent the rest of the evening visiting by the fire. Graff gave the mosquitos their quieting medicine and soon we were all in the tent, and the flap was fastened with a safety pin. "*Safety first always.*" After a short time, all the others were sleeping, but to me, the hours passed slowly by as I lay *thinking, thinking.*

These pretty little kittens have been my companions a good many hours during our stay at Londo Lake. Once they learned they could get some scraps of leftover fried fish, they seemed to make our place their new home.

Wednesday, August 2, 1922

We all got up early and had our breakfast. Yesterday, our camping neighbor Albert Cobb told Graff if he wanted to go picking huckleberries, he would go with us today out on the plains where he thought we would find lots of them.

So, we hustled around and I put up our lunch basket, while Lucille and Gladys made up the cots and washed up the dishes. Finally, we heard Albert toot his horn and we gathered our provisions and all entered the Ford. Graff let Albert take the lead with the Buick and off we went.

A little way down the road, Graff felt like having a race and passed Albert unexpectedly. *Now that wasn't fair.* Ha ha. Then he fell back into the rear place, just before we came upon a new little lake.

We soon hit the plains and passed a sign for National Boundary Line and saw the first telephone pole. *My, that seems home-like.* Then, at 9:30 a.m., Graff called out, "See the High Rollway!" and he soon stopped the car and we all got out. I was anxious to go down to the spring 260 feet below with Gladys and see if she could run all the way back up without resting, as she said she could.

So, Henry, Graff, Gladys, and I descended, followed by the Cobb youngsters; Ilene and Cleo. Upon reaching the bottom, we got a good drink of the cool spring water and fussed around for a few minutes. Lucille stayed at the top, standing in readiness to take a picture of us if she got the chance. The boys were ready to start back up the long, steep climb, so away we went. But Gladys found out: *tis easier said than done,* and a little way up, she was just as glad to sit down and rest as I was.

After we all reached the top and had ample time to recover from our climb, at 10:50 a.m., we all got in the cars and left for a place Albert called: "Somewhere." Shortly after getting started, Albert took the wrong road at the right, and we had to back up a little farther, then go ahead and turn to the left.

A sermon could be preached on "Life and Detours"—going ahead and finding you're wrong, then turning around and going in another direction.

Isn't it fun to plunge into a winding trail through the woods, not knowing whither it leads but going ahead on pure faith that you will get *somewhere, sometime?* What a splendid chance to help and be helped. What keen pleasure to drive the nose of the car into bottomless sand ruts and arrive at last with a boiling radiator and triumphant soul. And how good the good roads do seem when you strike them once more; *a paradise regained.*

What could be more beautiful than the woods with their green leaves and pretty ferns, the wild berries and crimson flowers? I wish we had a picture that would do it justice.

As we drove along, we noticed several times Henry had leaned forward in his seat, thinking in doing so he was helping the car to move out of the rut it was in. My, how we laughed. He said, "You never know, it might help."

At 10:03 a.m., Albert stopped the Buick, hopped out into the brush next to the car, and soon held up his hand with a big bunch of huckleberries in it. Graff smiled and said to him, "Dandy!"

We all got out and found just enough to eat as we went. As the picking didn't last long, we moved along a short distance farther. Then Albert pulled into a shady spot beside the road and announced, "We're here because we're here."

As all seemed anxious to eat, we brought forth the baskets and spread our blankets on the ground. Albert proceeded to build a nice little fire to roast the weenies. Our lunch consisted of bologna sandwiches, dill pickles, honey, cookies, hard-boiled eggs, and weenies. We washed down the good food with cold tea. Oh my, but it did taste good!

When I asked someone to pass the eggs to Albert, he said, "Yes, I like them, but never eat them when I'm camping."

But Lillie was game and said, "Well, I'll eat them anytime and will eat one now." And so on it went with our jolly neighbors, and we all had a good laugh.

After our picnic, we all headed back to the cars and reached Hale at 2:03 p.m. Graff parked the car at the barbershop and went in to get a shave and haircut.

As we waited in the car, the sky grew darker, and we heard the heavy roll of thunder. Henry had gone over to the post office and when he returned, he was fussing over the approaching storm. He went and told Graff that we ought to get started. Graff was just finishing his haircut and said, "It *hain't* going to storm yet."

Then Henry answered, "All right, take your time." And he did, as he waited for Albert to get shaved. Finally, the boys hustled out and got into the cars and we sped away. *Whew, how our driver drives!* Perhaps he was afraid that the two quarts of ice cream would melt before he got us home.

Safely back at See All Cottage at 3:00 p.m. just ahead of a big storm, which later passed over us to the north. We invited Albert and family over to eat ice cream and huckleberries. Later, we had a warm supper and spent the early evening quietly visiting around the fire. I will surely miss these peaceful moments we've spent here. We all decided to go to bed earlier than common, for we felt we had a long ride ahead of us on the morrow. *Let's not forget this was our last "good-night" at Londo Lake.*

Thursday, August 3, 1922

Henry and Graff awoke at 6:00 a.m. and were up and dressed. Soon the rest of us followed their example. We had a "spare-rib breakfast," scarcely able to find enough to satisfy our hunger. Then as the others went out to fish one last time, I called on the Noonans at Mosquito Point.

I carefully rubbed liniment on Mrs. Noonan's ankle and wrapped it for the last time. She was definitely improved and was grateful for my assistance. I had enjoyed being her "nurse" while we were camping neighbors. After I was done with caring for her injury, I went back to our tent and began to pack up things and got them in readiness for the homeward trip.

The fisherfolks returned, and Henry and Lucille came up with a pail of bluegills. Graff and Gladys came in a little later with thirty-five! The boys got busy and cleaned the fish to take home with us. Then Henry, Lucille, and I loaded Abner the trailer. It seemed we were going home with more than we came with.

The Noonan family came up to see us and say good-bye. Then Graff and Henry pulled the stakes and took down the tent. Lucille wanted a picture of us and the friends we were to leave behind. She quickly gathered them together and said, "Line up."

At 1:00 p.m., we extended hearty handshakes and the wish that we may all meet again. Then, with our belongings snugly packed, we all got into the car and Graff said, "All ready."

We waved good-bye to our friends, and we were on our way down the hill toward "Old Londo Lake" and along its pleasant shore. There was no sign of any mud or water in the roadway as we went past the old log building and on toward Bay City.

At 1:45 p.m., we went over the roughest piece of road and made it through without getting stuck. I noticed some older log buildings and mentioned I thought they looked like summer cottages. But Graff replied, "No, they are old lumber camps built fifty years ago."

At 2:00 p.m., we pulled into the little town of Nester. Graff stopped by the store, and we went inside to buy something for our dinner. We came out and found a nearby shady spot under a tall tree. I spread out our lunch of fresh bread, butter, sardines, cheese, cookies, and my pail of cold tea. We all sat down on the grass and enjoyed our lunch immensely.

Henry was fussing again over the big storm that seemed to be coming our way. With a concerned look on his face, he said, "Unless we hurry, this storm will surely hit us." It did look black and angry, but we finished our dinner, then Graff had to pump up one of the tires.

Finally, we were ready to head out again, keeping an eye on the storm clouds. After driving a distance, the storm seemed it wanted to go another direction, and we all breathed a sigh of relief.

At 3:40 p.m., I asked Graff to stop at a schoolhouse to get some water from their pump. While there, a car pulled up and inquired of Graff, "Do you know the way to Londo Lake?" He happily gave them directions and wished them well on their fishing trip.

We arrived in Standish at 4:00 p.m. at the county courthouse. *I shall always remember just how the courthouse looked.*

Graff went in again to see if his "bill book" had been found, but it had not. He soon came out with his marriage certificate in his hand. Gladys gave him a big smile when she saw it.

We entered Bay City on State Street at 5:27 p.m. *Biff.* There goes a tire, and we all got out. The boys soon got it patched and on we continued. After a three-minute ride, we turned on Litchfield St. and *biff* went another tire! We got out again and surely must have looked like a band of gypsies.

Graff assured us, "Never mind, we'll be on our way in a minute." So we girls contented ourselves by sitting down on the curb and watching the boys hustle. It seemed as though about half the people in Bay City were going by just at that time. Well, laugh if you want, we knew we had been camping, whether anyone else knew or not.

The boys were nearly done, and Lucille stood by with Kodak in hand and wondered if she should try for a picture. I motioned for her to hurry, for it was getting nearer sundown every minute. She quickly pressed the button, and this is what she got.

It doesn't seem just right to get a man when his back is turned, but we just had to do it.

On we went over past Winona Park, the Grand Trunk Railroad Depot, the fire department, and *safe at last*, at Graff's home at 6:15 p.m. He jumped out and unlocked the garage. The girls got out, quickly took the key and ran for the house, unlocked the back door, and went inside. We all got busy sorting out and carrying their belongings inside.

Gladys started the oil stove and put the teakettle on, as Graff went back to the Ford and headed to the store. We all got washed and brushed up a bit and felt lots better and ready to help Gladys with the supper. I looked over some of the huckleberries we brought back and soon we had everything ready. Graff insisted on our having supper in the new dining room. He said, "We've not eaten a meal in there yet, and I want you folks to eat with us there the first time."

So we girls set the table and when all were seated, Henry said grace, thanking God for the privilege of being with these friends in this, their new home.

After a lovely meal, Graff and Lucille went into the parlor to listen to some music together on his new Victrola. No more need to "crank it up" to be able to enjoy it, with this dandy electric model.

Gladys and I were about to clear away the remains of supper when her sister Enid, husband Frank and family came in. The little girl with the black eye helped us, and she was a hustler.

During our visit and while Graff used the fly swatter to good advantage, the electric lights went out. He and Frank discovered the fuse had burned out. Graff found a new one and put it in. Frank brought in the old one for us to see "how hot it is." Shortly after 11:00 p.m., Enid took the sleeping babies, and they all went home.

We went out in the kitchen, and I found that Gladys had forgotten to heat up her red raspberries that had "worked" while we were gone camping. I told her, "We must not leave them till morning, for if we do, they won't keep." So, I got the stew kettle on the stove, Graff brought the sugar, and I put on good supply over the berries. We soon have them cooked and ready to go back in the jars again.

Then Our Five thought it was about time to retire. We ordered one of our cots brought in for Lucille and placed in our bedroom. I had been used to having *bodyguards* and felt safer with someone nearby. Gladys brought out a big feather bed to put on the cot, and I soon had a comfortable place fixed up for Lucille to sleep.

The night was very warm, and I soon decided I'd be more comfortable on the floor; so I took my pillow and slipped quietly down on the floor where I finally dropped off to sleep until 2:00 a.m. Then, I got back into bed where I rested until 7:00 a.m. when we heard Graff stirring around in the kitchen. Henry dressed and went out, and soon Lucille and I got up, too.

Friday, August 4, 1922

At 8:30 a.m., the girls had breakfast ready. While we were at the breakfast table, Graff said, "Our living here will make it better for us on our next trip. For now, we can stop here and rest going up and the same coming back from Londo Lake." *Yes, Laddie, that will be quite handy in the years to come, Lord willing.*

After breakfast, the boys went downtown to purchase new inner tubes, which they put on the Ford when they got back. Gladys and I washed the dishes, and I fixed up my room. Lucille and her father went to the store and bought some buns and cookies for me to take home.

At 11:05 a.m., the house was locked, and we girls got in the car. Graff got in and we backed out, while we waited for Henry to go pump some water for the radiator. At last, he had it and away we went.

Shortly after we passed through Munger at 11:35 a.m., Lucille hollered, "There goes the trailer!" But Graff didn't hear her, and I called to him to stop as Lucille looked back and said, "Good-bye, *Abner.*"

One glance from Gladys and she yelled, "Hold her, Newt, she's rearing!" And over it went into the ditch.

Well, it is needless to try to explain what we were all thinking as we got out and went back. We thought, of course, that it would be a complete wreck. Two cars passed us and then pulled over to the side of the road. The good men came back to our assistance, and one of them said, “We’re from Sanilac County and maybe we will want some help before we get back home.” Our “Good Samaritans” looked over our wreck as Lucille was on the job and got a picture at once.

Graff had gone across the road where there was a threshing machine outfit in the barnyard, expecting to get some help, but Henry called to him and said, “With these men to help us, we can pull it out all right.” So he came back with a big heavy rope he had found and all lent a hand. Soon we had the trailer up on the roadside. The poor old trailer and contents looked pretty well shaken up.

This piece of timber is what Graff got for a new tongue.

While Henry was fussing and we were all looking on, Lucille got this picture of the group.

Henry got busy trying to fasten the tongue to the Sedan. We girls sat in the car, and I began to sing,

"Home Sweet Home"
Mid pleasures and palaces though we may roam,
Be it ever so humble there's no place like home!
A charm from the skies seems to hallow us there,
Which seek through the world, is ne'er met with elsewhere.

At first, all that can be heard is my voice, then Henry joined in on the chorus.

Home! Home! Sweet, Sweet Home!
There's no place like Home!
There's no place like Home!

I continued singing the next verse, as the others in our group hummed along. We might as well sing and be merry, as these little mishaps all fill in on an auto trip.

It had been just one hour since we left Bay City. "Please have the cookies, everyone." I offered Graff one, but he declined. He did drink a cup of cold tea to steady his nerves.

Smash! Graff exclaimed, "Here's another wreck. I've tipped over your lunch basket, tin cups and all." I was surprised he could get his foot into a basket of that size.

With the trailer fixed and firmly tied to the car, we were moving along again. I tried to look at the pretty scenery to take my mind off all the mishaps.

At 12:20 p.m., "For goodness sake, there goes the trailer again!" I called out. Graff pulled over and after twenty-five minutes of fussing around, all was ready and with the man at the wheel, Gladys said, "Let 'er go!" And he surely did. We were just three miles from Gilford, when *whew, smell the tar, they have put that on since we went north.* Henry said to Graff he'd better stop and let him see if everything was all right. *Safety first.*

Graff asked, "What is it, another loose connection?" But Henry found that everything was okay. Good news, for we were all anxious to get going and soon were on the old road to Millington.

At 1:45 p.m., we arrived back at the Old Home safe and sound. We found Vilas, little Theo and Billy in the backyard. Willard came out to welcome us home and got a warm kiss from his mother. *I always say that they are never too old for that.*

We all loved on the babies and then entered the old home once more, where hurriedly preparations were soon started for getting us a warm dinner. We cooked potatoes, fried eggs, fish, raisin bread and butter, green onions, blackberry pie, (a donation from Thalia) and some good hot tea.

As we all sat down to our much-anticipated meal, Lucille said, "Home sweet home!"

Chapter 19
Wait to Greet

Friday, August 4, 1922

Well, we were all ready and sat down to the table at last. I thought it seemed rather strange to have things quite so handy to cook with instead of a campfire. But I lived through it and, like the others, ate a good big dinner.

While we were eating, son John came down to see us and visited while we ate. We told him of some of our adventures we just had at Londo Lake. We all said we had a good time, but twas good to be back home.

After dinner, Henry went outside to look the garden over and see if everything had been kept in shape while we were gone. Gladys asked Lucille to go up town with her to buy some brown silk hose, and off they went.

Graff went into the parlor to lay down on the couch, and a few minutes later, I went in quietly, expecting to find him sleeping, but he was wide awake and said, "Come in, sit down and rest." As I felt a little tired, I took his advice and sat there and visited with him.

We spoke of what the future had in store for him and Gladys and how I hoped to see their love for each other grow more and more. I told him how I had tried to give Gladys some helpful hints.

I explained, "Graff, you will never know what this trip has meant to me. I've had over thirty years of experience in housekeeping and different things, and yet it was no little task for me to take her in my arms as I did up at Londo Lake and try to tell her the things that might be of greatest benefit to her. I felt she was doubly dear to me, and I've tried to help her in many ways. I know too how kind and good you can be and many little things you can do to make her happy if you are careful and thoughtful as I know you can be."

Graff sat up and said softly, "Gladys will never forget your kindness, and you will never be sorry you went to Londo Lake this year." I nodded and felt a sweet sense of affection for both of them.

Just then, Henry came in with his face all black and dirty, so I tried to get him to wash up and come in to visit with us. But he said, "No, not till I get Graff's car swept out."

The girls finally came back from town and went upstairs, took off their dress skirts, and lay down to have a short nap and rest.

I went and cleared the table and fixed up things in the kitchen. Then I went into the parlor again and drew the curtains down so the flies wouldn't disturb Graff. Poor fellow, let him get a little rest if he can. This homeward trip had been a trying one for him, but regardless of storms, blowouts, and trailer trouble, he was a good old scout and came through on the home stretch with a smile.

After a while, he came out with that tired expression gone, and I knew he had enjoyed his short rest, for there was a peaceful look on his face.

He asked, "Where is Gladys? We must get ready to go, for I want to stop and see Ollie at Vassar a few minutes." So, I called the girls and they got up, put their dresses on, and came downstairs.

Henry wanted Graff to have some plums from our trees, so the boys and I went to the garden and picked half a bushel for him. With basket in hand, Henry carried the plums out to the car.

Soon Gladys was ready, and we all went through the kitchen and out to the south driveway where in the same old place the Ford Sedan was parked.

Graff entered the car first and took his place behind the wheel. I stepped up for my good-bye kiss and then I kissed Gladys. One by one, the others said their good-byes while I thanked Graff for the happy hours we spent with him and Gladys on this trip.

Then, Gladys took her place in the front seat and the big Laddie backed the car out of the driveway. He let Gladys take the wheel, and they were on their way heading toward the west and passed from our sight at 5:00 p.m.

As I entered the house and sat down, my thoughts went out to them as I followed them on their way back to their own cozy home. Methinks I can see them as they unlock the back door and enter their new life alone once more. And as the days go by, I wonder what their next letter will bring to me. I suppose it will be full of the joy of home life, perhaps telling me of a trip up to the old home at Midland, or to some other far away city they have visited. And I shall read it with a feeling of thankfulness that it is so.

Perhaps, some might wonder why I feel as I do. But these two, whose lives have been joined together, know and understand why they are so dear to me, and that is enough.

I shall look for my letters to come from them, and no other will follow them day after day with more fervent prayer that their lives may be shaped to each other's need and comfort as I will do. I'll look forward to them coming to us at times so we may all enjoy a good time together.

Some of the happiest hours of his life have been spent with me and mine, and now we will always be glad to see them drive up and come in at any time to visit us.

My task is done, my book complete
and closed is lying at my feet.
I will not say, "Good-bye"
But rather, "wait to greet"
The dear ones that I always love to meet.

THE END

Postscript

A poem attributed to Ethel Van Wagnen written in her handwriting and not dated.

Shadows

Do you sit and look in the shadows
for a form you cannot see?
Do you know that back in the darkness
she is thinking and longing for thee?

Do you know that when twilight deepens,
on the land and on the sea;
that with hands meekly folded,
she is still thinking of thee?

And again when night has settled,
and in the quiet gloom;
methinks she still can see you,
in your still and darkened room.

Where with hands extended,
reaching for the one you love the best.
Who will come and silently bending,
press a kiss upon your lips.

Do you know how sad and lonely
she has been for many years?
How her heart has nearly broken
while she smiled, to hide the tears?

Then dear, always remember
that wherever you may be;
her thots, her love is always with you,
for she thinks of you constantly.

And sometimes you will remember
how your lips have pressed her own.
How you clasped her to you gently,
then you each passed on alone.

And perhaps someday up yonder,
God will call his own.
And you'll meet to part no never,
there beside the Great White Throne.

Afterword

Notes from Linda

- Henry and Ethel were married for sixty-nine years and both lived long lives: Henry died May 28, 1962 at the age of ninety-one years, and Ethel died April 29, 1968 at the age of ninety-four years.
- Through researching this book, I discovered that at the time of their marriage in 1922, Graff was fifty-two years and Gladys was seventeen years old. That was quite a surprising age difference, yet nothing was ever mentioned about it in Ethel's writings. The only reference that she made was where she talked to Graff and Gladys in the tent and said, "*You remind me of two children in one way, in another tis more than child's play, when you think of the future.*"
- Graff and Gladys had their first child the year after the vacation in 1922. This appeared to be the end of the combined camping trips to Londo Lake despite their plans for the next year. The couple had six children and were married twenty-five years when Graff died in 1947 at the age of seventy-seven years. Gladys was forty-two years old when she was widowed and lived until 1988 when she died at the age of eighty-three years.
- Henry and Ethel never owned or drove a car. Lucille (as mentioned in the journals) at age twenty was learning to drive with Graff as her teacher.
- Henry and Ethel were asked to sing at many funerals. This information was obtained from another journal that documented each deceased name, date, and what songs were sung such as: "The Old Rugged Cross," "The Beautiful Garden of Prayer," "The Eastern Gate," "Some Time We'll Understand," and "He Sleeps in the Valley of Peace." At times, Ethel sang solos or had duets with Henry or another lady. They also sang in the church choir at the Methodist-Episcopal Church in Millington.

- Henry served as Millington Township Supervisor for twenty-one years. (Note: mention of tax rolls in book)
- Henry was a life member of the Masons and International Order of the Odd Fellows (IOOF). Ethel and Lucille continued their participation in the Rebekahs throughout their lives. It appears that the family involvement with the Masons, Odd Fellows, and Rebekahs lodges were mainly focused on community service and social activities.
- Lucille was known to me as *Grandma Throop*. After her death in 1973 at the age of seventy-four years, a beautiful article about her was printed in the *Tuscola County Advertiser*. It was also read by Lila DeBoer on her local radio program where, after telling of her many ways of helping people and serving the needy, she referred to Lucille as the "Angel of Millington."
- The Methodist-Episcopal Church mentioned in Ethel's writings and Chapter 15 (in 1892) is the same church where my parents, Donald and Norma Gee, were married on January 31, 1948. They raised five children and had been married sixty-eight years when my mother died on October 30, 2016. Her memorial service was held in the rebuilt church building, which still contains a display of historical records and memorabilia of the Van Wagnen family and many of their descendants. Less than four months after we gathered for my mother's memorial service, my father died on February 22, 2017. During the finishing process of publishing this book I lost both of my parents, but it was a blessing to me to have been able to share many parts of *Golden Memories* with them before they died. Among Dad's last words were his confession of faith in Jesus Christ, and the bittersweet words, "I miss your mother." Even though our family will miss them both in ways we haven't yet imagined, it is comforting to know that they have been reunited in heaven.

Donald and Norma Gee ~ January 31, 1948
"Until death do us part"

Millington Methodist Church ~ "You may kiss the bride"

- In my research of the Bailey family (Ethel's father's side), I was able to trace back thirty-one generations to Count Siher (Henry L.) O'Bailey, who was born in France in the year 990. There were several generations of counts and countesses in Normandy, France, and then fifteen generations of sirs and ladies in England in the years 1076 to 1575. Two Baileys were knighted; two died in Israel during the Crusades, and Sir Robert Bailey II was a member of the British Parliament circa 1440. Of course, all this information needs to be further documented, but it was a fascinating search.
- My search of the Van Wagnen family ancestry was very productive, finding roots in the Netherlands. In Chapter 15, Henry's father Irvin Van Wagnen tells some actual family history with his stories. The name was taken from the town his ancestors left in Wageningen, Holland, and adapted and shortened to Van (from the town of) Wagenen. The family history and following pictures are also nicely documented in the book entitled:

Dutch Houses in the Hudson Valley Before 1776
By Helen Wilkinson Reynolds

The valley of the Rondout, Ulster County, at Wagen Dal, a locality settled by the Van Wagenen family before 1700. This stream here is narrow, the dale secluded. One of the homesteads of the Van Wagenens occupies the foreground.

The house of Jacob Aertson Van Wagenen

One of five stone houses at Wagen Dal on the Rondout, all homesteads of the Van Wagenen family. The front portion of the house shown is cut with the date: 1699; the rear is undated but early. A descendant of Jacob Aertson Van Wagenen still owned and occupied the house in 1928.

Also discovered through ancestry researches was a copy of the handwritten (in Dutch) account in the family Bible of Jacob Aertson Van Wagenen. It contains the family history beginning in 1652 and records the births and deaths of his fifteen children and the first five generations of his family.

On May 18, 2013, at the age of eighty-three, my mother Norma Gee visited the house of her grandparents (Henry and Ethel Van Wagnen) at 8461 East Street, in Millington, Michigan, where I took this picture. She had lived there from ages four to eight after the divorce of her parents. Although she did not enter the house, she recalled many happy memories there and drew a sketch of the inside of the house, its furnishings, and the backyard. These details were helpful to me in describing scenes of how the rooms actually looked in 1921.

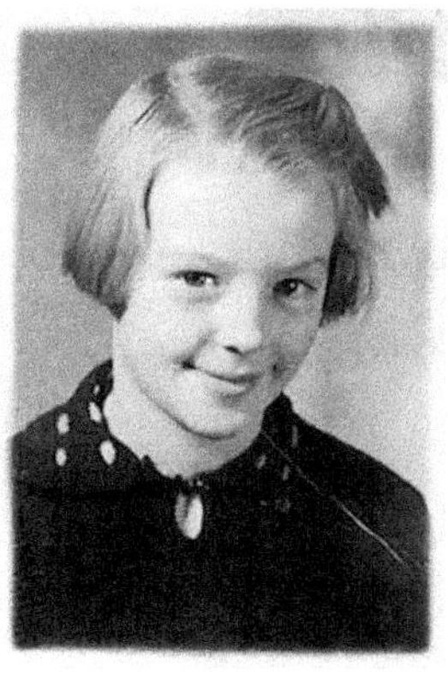

Norma Jean Griffin,
Eight years old
November 1938

These side-by-side pictures show Ethel in the span of seventy-five years.

Ethel Bailey
Circa September, 1892
Nineteen years old, near her birthday and wedding to Henry.

Ethel Van Wagnen
September 16, 1967
Taken on her last birthday at the age of ninety-four years.

For more pictures and historical information, visit the website:
www.goldenmemoriesbook.com

Finally, after reading all the entries in the original journals, questions may still arise as to the relationship of Ethel and Graff. I would like to include these comments by my friend and author Karen Conover, who after reading the journals concluded the following:

"I honestly don't believe there was an illicit, physical relationship between Ethel and Graff, although today's reader might erroneously jump on that idea. They did, no doubt however, love each other deeply. He represented a wonderful and cherished time in her life (and her first love). She represented the world of love and security (and innocence) that he knew before the death of his mother... and then his wife. Their bond was, I believe, greater than their bonds of marriage. But their spouses and her children knew this bond and accepted it generously because they sensed its purity."

I end this book with the hope that I have done my best to search out information and clues to my great-grandmother's life. In doing so, I feel "Grandma Van" is better known to me than before. I was also able to share new discoveries of family history with my mother, and that has been a blessing to me.

God has extended his gift of love and grace to us, "in that while we were yet sinners, Christ died for us." The grace we receive can and should be passed along to others.

I have attempted to write *Golden Memories* with that grace toward Ethel and Graff. No matter how much searching is done, we will never know all the details of their lives.

And that, I believe, is how it should be.

for the Lord sees not as man sees;
man looks on the outward appearance,
but the Lord looks on the heart.
—1 Samuel 16:7b (RSV)

Resources

Michigan census data, newspaper archives, death certificates, plat maps: Midland County Clerk, The Old Nest: Photoplay Magazine 1921, Family archives used by permission.

Photos: Wagon Dal–Valley of the Rondout & House of Jacob Aertson Van Wagenen from the book: *Dutch Houses in the Hudson Valley Before 1776* by Helen Wilkinson Reynolds

Unless otherwise indicated, all Scripture quotations are taken from *The Holy Bible, King James Version,* now in public domain.

[Scripture quotations are] from the Revised Standard Version of the Bible, copyright © 1946, 1952, and 1971 the Division of Christian Education of the National Council of the Churches of Christ in the United States of America. Used by permission. All rights reserved.

Hymns: *What a Friend We Have in Jesus* - Joseph M. Scriven & Charles C. Converse -1855 *Jesus Paid It All* - Elvina M. Hall & John T. Grape – 1865 Methodist Episcopal Hymnal

Songs: *Let the Rest of the World Go By*
Words by J. Keirn Brennan–Music by Ernest R. Ball
Leave Me With A Smile
Words and Music By: Chas. Koehler and Earl Burtnett–1911
Home! Sweet Home!
Lyricist: John Howard Payne–Composer: Henry Rowley Bishop
Angry Words
Words and music by Horatio R. Palmer

Quote –Chapter 6: *(You may break, You may shatter the vase, if you will, But the scent of the roses will hang round it still.)* by Thomas Moore

CPSIA information can be obtained
at www.ICGtesting.com
Printed in the USA
BVHW011143170519
548614BV00004B/52/P

9 781640 793866